Advance Praise for
If an Egyptian Cannot Speak English

"*If an Egyptian Cannot Speak English* seethes with metaphoric passion and emotional intelligence beneath its piecrust of metafictional playfulness, and will reward every rereading with new doses of pleasure. Noor Naga's writing is fearless, virtuosic, and pithy with aphorism, her sentences honed to dagger point, thrumming with swag. This is a writer who looks and listens with an assiduous, sensual attention, and whose voice, in this engrossing debut novel, has found a subject to make it sing."

—A. Igoni Barrett, judge's statement

"In *If an Egyptian Cannot Speak English,* Noor Naga finds a form for diasporic consciousness: capacious enough to hold conflicting voices, inventive enough to capture the dream state of life in translation, supple enough to express varieties of heartbreak at the margins of culture. Through a love story told at a breathless pace, Naga evokes breath: the presence of living bodies, whose silence surrounds all novels, never quite caught on the page. This is a book for anyone who's ever been mesmerized by language, amazed and stricken by what it can and cannot do." —Sofia Samatar

"Through exquisite invention and a tightly woven form, Noor Naga brings us into the colliding spaces of cultural duality met by the perennial struggles of people attempting to reconcile with one another and themselves. With the backdrop of a Cairo in perpetual chaos and the aftermath of the Egyptian revolution, here are two young Egyptians, each from one side of the Atlantic, trying to find meaning amidst a conception of nation and belonging that seems to have all but dissipated. Beyond attempting to come to terms with one's identity, these nameless characters are in search of revelation. *If an Egyptian Cannot Speak English* is fixated on complexities that define how we come to understand ourselves, and our striving to grapple with desire and yearning while also being beholden to one another. Enthralling and nuanced, this is a novel by a writer whose powers are just becoming known." **—Matthew Shenoda**

"Noor Naga's language combines precision with extraordinary suggestiveness. Reading this book is like stepping through an open doorway and realizing that a sparkling zodiac of colorful expressions lies another small step away. One has the impulse to keep going and to stop only to wave someone else to hurry along."

—Ato Quayson

IF AN EGYPTIAN CANNOT SPEAK ENGLISH

Also by Noor Naga

Washes, Prays

IF AN EGYPTIAN CANNOT SPEAK ENGLISH

A Novel

Noor Naga

Graywolf Press

Page 30 contains an adaptation of a line from Gloria Steinem's *Outrageous Acts and Everyday Rebellions* (1983).

All best efforts have been made to secure permission to reproduce the lyrics from "Humble" by Kendrick Lamar that appear on page 119.

An excerpt of this book first appeared in *Granta* as "American Girl and Boy from Shobrakheit."

The author acknowledges support of the Canada Council for the Arts.

This publication is made possible, in part, by the voters of Minnesota through a Minnesota State Arts Board Operating Support grant, thanks to a legislative appropriation from the arts and cultural heritage fund. Significant support has also been provided by the McKnight Foundation, the Lannan Foundation, the Amazon Literary Partnership, and other generous contributions from foundations, corporations, and individuals. To these organizations and individuals we offer our heartfelt thanks.

Canada Council
for the Arts

Conseil des arts
du Canada

CLEAN
WATER
LAND &
LEGACY
AMENDMENT

MINNESOTA
STATE ARTS BOARD

Published by Graywolf Press
212 Third Avenue North, Suite 485
Minneapolis, Minnesota 55401

www.graywolfpress.org

Published in the United States of America

ISBN 978-1-64445-081-9

Library of Congress Control Number: 2021940565

Cover design: Kimberly Glyder

Cover art: Jean-Léon Gérôme, *Bishari, Bust of a Warrior,* 1872

إلى أطفال الضفادع

"I am not what you think I am. You are what you think I am."

—Instagram caption by @hanaperlas, November 5, 2016

PART ONE

QUESTION: If you don't have anything nice to say, should your mother be punished?

And then Mother placed a single peach on a saucer at the center of the table. With a carving knife, divided it in four. *Dinner*, she said. My grandmother, whose perfect teeth were singly stolen by a dentist working from his one-room across the river and seating patients on the bed he sleeps in, took all the peach quarters and squished them into her ears. *Such greed*, said Mother, sucking the hollow seed. Father breathed. Swinging her elbows like a racewalker, Grandmother busied into the kitchen and climbed inside the stove. The next day they placed her collection of paper cranes into the ground with her, so I left. This was ten years ago. The distance from Shobrakheit to Cairo is 140 kilometers. I took a microbus, then the train.

QUESTION: Is it arrogant to return to a place you've never been?

If I was a white girl with a shaved head, they probably wouldn't have cared. But because I was an Egyptian girl with a shaved head, they wouldn't let me forget it. Everything was fine at JFK. Even when four hundred Egyptians funneled into a Boeing 777 destined for Cairo, no one noticed me. For twelve hours our heads nodded, lolled against one another as we dozed and dreamed, and there was no telling in the canned gloom who was who. Then the lights came on and we landed. These same four hundred passengers disembarking on the other side seemed to have forgotten where we'd come from. They glared openly at me and muscled past in the aisle, suspicious all of a sudden. No one helped me get my backpack from the overhead bin. At passport control, the officer looked like a younger version of my father. Slender, brown, and long-faced, with silver glasses that gave him a pained, glittering look of sensitivity. Behind me the line was long and vocal, but he held my American passport leisurely in his hands, as if it were a book he had read before. He said my name, searched my face the way strangers study the daughters of a niqab-wearing woman, noting the texture of their hair, the pucker of their mouths, aging the children's faces in their minds, searching for the mother's beauty. It was clear that the officer was picturing me with hair. He was searching for the Egyptian in me, or possibly the illness. I wanted to say, *Same.* I had filled out the boxes on the declaration form in a child's handwriting, articulating the tooth of every letter *sin* and dotting my diacritics individually. The effect was neat but painstaking. *What brings you here?* he asked in Arabic. *Do you have an Egyptian passport?* I shook my head. *National ID card?* I said, *Pardon?* He sent me out of the line and around the corner to another man, who was very large, with purple eye rings, smoking cigarettes in a glass cubicle. He looked trapped in it, as if on display in a museum.

This man finished his cigarette, brushing through my passport with his thumb before asking in English, *How long you stay?* I tried to tell him I was staying for good. *Six months, okay?* he asked and I nodded because his English was poor but my Arabic was poorer. He made a loop and a dash on a pink slip. *Take this, go that office up the stair, you pay, you come again here.* I went up the stairs to the second office and there was no one there. When I returned to the man in the glass case, he shouted over his shoulder in Arabic, *Dina! Go tell that son of a shoe to sit at the cashier!* and shooed me with the back of his hand before I could explain. The son of a shoe looked about fourteen, with matching purple eye rings, smiling. I paid him and returned to the smoking man, who sent me back to the passport control line with a paper visa in my hand. *Hey, American! Come here!* It was the officer from before, the one who looked like my father, calling me to the front. All the other Egyptians glared at me as I moved apologetically up the queue. I wanted to explain that I was one of them, that I had been in line earlier and paid my dues, but my Arabic . . . The officer stamped my passport, winked, and let me through.

QUESTION: If your mother wanted to feed you forever, why would she cut the cord?

After my grandmother's death by oven, I knew I would leave Shobrakheit for good. During the last conversation I had with mother, I said, *I'm going to Cairo.* She sat tenderly supergluing the sole of her shoe back onto the heel. From behind her focus she mumbled, *Cairo, Cairo . . . is that beyond the pigeon tower?* I said, *Yes.* Her eyes watered from the chemical smell. *Son, is it beyond the hospital across the river?* I said, *Yes*, and then added, *It's even beyond Damanhour. What?* she gasped. *And there are people beyond Damanhour?* I hoisted a corn bag of clothes over my shoulder, the camera swinging around my neck. She lifted a hand to smooth back her hair, and the shoe, now glued to her thumb, went with it. Bloodied her eye. I took a microbus from Shobrakheit to Damanhour and the fog was so thick we could not see even the dashed road lines. The driver steered with his whole head out the window. There was no one in the white air but us. I cried into my corn bag. For days after my grandmother cooked herself to death, Mother didn't say it, but we knew anyway that she was sour from thinking: *Shame to waste the gas and not eat.* The whole village knew she was wondering how best to divide a peach into thirds. From Damanhour, I took the train to Cairo and inside it the air was very brown, like closet air. I fell asleep and woke up with a man feeling my thigh through my torn pocket. People think anyone with a camera will have coins instead of skin in his pocket. When I arrived at Ramses Station in Cairo, the air was people. Nowhere you looked wasn't people. They clogged every street and then piled on top of each other in buildings twenty stories high. Many were not even Egyptian. You could turn into an alley and find fifty Sudanese men, bluer than black, with cheeks like shoulder blades and ankles like knives, or else women as tall as

I am, women so pale you could see rivered blood at their wrists and neck. I heard twenty Arabics in my first week and wherever I went people asked me—sometimes in English because of the hair—*Where you from?* While one man was asking me this, another whizzing by on motorcycle stole a cigarette right out of my hand. While waiting my turn to order a sandwich, I saw children in school uniforms drowning kittens in a barrel of tar. A waitress my mother's age came up to me, clicking gum with an open mouth: *I like tall boys like you—don't you want to kiss me?* My first year in Cairo, I still spoke country, referring to myself in the plural. *We do*, I answered. She laughed in my face. Led me by the hand to a garage, where she ran her tongue along my teeth and rubbed my knees. I was nineteen. This was ten years ago, 2007, and since then I have been home only once. Somewhere in Shobrakheit, my mother is dividing all the dinner fruits in half.

QUESTION: If the stampede is heading toward you, should you turn around and run?

What they really want to know is whether my head is shaved because I have cancer or because I'm a pervert. Instead of this question they ask another. *What brings you here?* I get it from all of them: the driver who picked me up from the airport with my name on cardboard, the one who works for my mother's former classmate Sherry; the Faiyumi doorman of the building downtown, who took my bags up without asking, against my protests; Madame Fadya, the cleaning lady, who was waiting in the apartment to hand over the keys; then a few days later Sherry herself, a woman with a moist, cosmetically bloated face who lives in Zamalek with her two tiny dogs. She is one of those desperate women, like my mother, who, the more effort they put into their appearance, the older they look. We sat on her balcony while a Sudanese maid came and went with tea, then sablé and petits fours, then red and white wine, and I squirmed at the horror of being served by a Black woman with a kerchief tied around her head. *What brings you to Cairo, dear?* Sherry asked, but before I could tell her, she had moved on. *I haven't seen your mother since eighty-nine, you know that? I don't blame her. It's not a good time to be here. A few years ago, okay, I could understand. Post-revolution, everyone was coming back all excited. Ask me where they are now.* I looked at her blankly. She made pedaling cycles with her cigarette hand until I recited: *Where are they now?* Then she continued as though I hadn't. *Twenty pounds to the dollar. This is the exchange rate today. A year ago, it was eight. Tell your mother I miss her.* The resemblance between them was uncanny, actually: the same vanity, the femme fatalism, the overpowering smell of creams and powders. You just knew she spent too much time alone in front of mirrors, crying. I had not spoken to my mother since I left New York, where she'd been grilling me almost hourly: *Why are you going there?* Now that I have *gone there*, the question has folded on itself, put a foot in its mouth: *Why have you come here?* This is the first thing people ask when they meet me, and their tone is more indignant than inquisitive. The more they discover, the more offended they are. *You live in America? Have American passport? Do you know what people here would give for an American passport? We are all trying to leave and you have the option to be there but instead—why are you here?* I try to explain that America is not heaven, that there are problems everywhere. *Trump*, I say, but it is the wrong thing to say, to the driver, to the doorman. Madame Fadya, the cleaning lady, was the only one who believed me, and seemed pleased to hear it. *The people are warmer here, kinder, more humane*, I continued, as though I had been in Cairo for longer than four hours when I met her and could possibly have an opinion. She was excited by this, wanted me to elaborate, which I did. *Egyptians are warmer*, she repeated after me when I was done, and her relief was palpable, as if I had confirmed a private fantasy she'd been cultivating for years. *I've never been interested in traveling outside, myself. Some of my brothers work in Saudi, they always say it is cleaner outside and the money's good, but I've never wanted to leave. No place is better than any other, we only think it is.* I agreed with Madame Fadya initially—she was agreeing with me, after all—but the longer she spoke, the more uncomfortable I grew. I started to think she was gullible and dim-witted for treating my account without skepticism. After all, I was skeptical myself. Why *was* I in Cairo? When I first told my father I was going to Cairo, he changed the subject, pretended not to have heard me. A few days later I called him at the office in Midtown because he so rarely came home anymore. He cleared his throat as though fatherhood had just been declared carcinogenic and he wanted nothing to do with it: he was doing a cleanse, he was detoxing, he had given up gluten and dairy and daughters. *Venus is in retrograde*, he said.

We feel a strong impulse to break out of cycles we've been trapped in for years. Moving across the Atlantic may not be the answer, though. When I pressed him about his own running—from his marriage, from his family—he said with finality, *I can't make this decision for you.* Which was typical. My mother was no more helpful. *I've decided to go to Cairo after graduation*, I told her from the other end of the tuxedo couch in our living room. *You really don't know what you're saying*, she snapped. The next morning at breakfast she began to cry. *You're leaving me? How can you leave me, with everything I'm going through?* A week later she became cruel. *Let me guess, let me guess*, she began to say every few hours, apropos of nothing. *You want to connect with your roots.* Two air quotes around the word *roots*. My parents left Cairo in the eighties and never looked back. When I arrived at the apartment on Mahmoud Bassiouny Street, I realized my mother had gone through my suitcase and removed all my sweatpants and short shorts and slides, adding a few dragging dresses still minty with the tags, and many shawls. This is her love language. She'd arranged everything: Sherry's driver to pick me up from the airport, an apartment sublet in my name downtown, a job for me at the British Council, teaching English. It couldn't have been easier, but it has not been easy.

QUESTION: How far can you run from home before you run out of water?

The first few years in Cairo were shit. I had a little money my grandmother had squirreled away for me. She used to crochet bridal doilies and sell them in Alexandria. All her life she told me I would eat from her hands one day, I would eat with this lace. And I did. On the microbus from Shobrakheit to Damanhour, I found four thousand pounds folded between my camera lens and its cap. When had she? The day of the oven, the day she . . . I cried into my corn bag. Someone sitting at the back called me a feeding horse. Someone else laughed. I thought I would die on that microbus in the clean white air. I thought I had cried until I fogged up all the roads going anywhere, that I'd never again see beyond my outstretched arms. Those first few years in Cairo, I lived off my grandmother's lacework and said a prayer for her every night. I enrolled at the University of Cairo in Mass Communications and made some money assisting cameramen on low-budget commercials and sometimes porn. It was hand-to-mouth for years, degrading, impossibly desolate. Then revolution.

QUESTION: Is science enough to explain why you see a mirage when you're dying of thirst?

I arrived in June. My first month in Cairo, I kept mistaking strangers for family. Everywhere I looked I saw my parents and my sister, Lulu. In the bars of downtown Cairo, especially Zigzag, any of the curly-haired girls with enormous, glassy doll-eyes could be Lulu. My mother was every hefty tante in tassel-fringe capris, pointed-toe mules, and my father was the same cricket-legged bald man serving me coffee, driving me home. In my first week of teaching English at the British Council, I even called one of my students *baba* by accident, to the class's uproarious delight. I'd never done anything like that before. When I told Sami about the incident, he quipped with oedipal reasoning that I must be in love with the student. Sami is the nephew of my program coordinator at the British Council, and I met him at Café Riche, downtown. He is blond, straight, overweight, with frameless glasses that were fashionable in the early 2000s but now aged him by two decades at least—a virgin. He introduced me to Reem (clearly gay, clearly smitten), and the two of them cheerfully adopted me. They were both pop culture junkies and conspirators whose fiery friendship was often mistaken for romance by the unimaginative clientele at Riche—sighing old ladies with their cheeks in their hands. To be fair, they were inseparable. The first day I met them, they were rehearsing an old debate over who had killed Soad Hosny. Reem was making chopping motions on the table with the edge of her hand, constructing a timeline using the salt and pepper shakers. Sami let her talk until she had climbed to a breathless climax before calmly introducing a hypothetical: *Why would Intelligence murder her in the most telltale way possible?* And Reem lost it. She stood up and began to shout, leaning over the table, using her whole body to gesticulate. *And I suppose you think Ashraf Marwan was suicidal too! If she* wanted to kill herself, why choose someone else's balcony? Why fly all the way to London? They killed her, they killed her in the exact same apartment complex in London where they killed Ashraf Marwan, because she was going to write her memoirs and expose them all. Witnesses saw men in suits throw Soad Hosny from the balcony, and— I waved a hand in front of Reem's face. Who's Soad Hosny? I asked. Reem's and Sami's faces sprang open simultaneously. They blinked. It was the nicest gift I could have given them. I'd never seen two people so horrified with joy. Oh, honey, said Reem, as though seeing me properly for the first time. She collapsed back into her chair. You know her, said Sami kindly. You know her for sure. She was in the sixties film Eshaet hob? I shook my head, but he kept nodding. You know her, you'd know her if you saw her. Khally balak min Zouzou? I shook my head, but they were both delighted. He opened up his laptop and we all watched Khally balak min Zouzou on YouTube, Sami pausing to point out the most iconic scenes while Reem looked up memes of the film, both of them singing along to the songs. The other customers stared at us and I thought we might be kicked out of Café Riche, but no one complained. I realized only as I came to leave that Sami's father was the owner, that no one who sat with Sami at the table ever paid, and that he himself never left that table. As long as the café was open, Sami had to be there, keeping an eye on the cashier and the servers and the guests, who he said tried to pocket the vintage Stella ashtrays whenever he went to the bathroom. He was twenty-one, smoking LM cigarettes, drinking beers from 10 a.m. to 10 p.m. in the same chair at the same table every day, bored out of his mind.

QUESTION: If everyone you knew jumped off a bridge, wouldn't you believe you could fly?

If you weren't there I can't tell you what it was like. To wake up from a dream you have been dreaming since birth is powerful. But to wake up from a dream you have been dreaming from birth *with almost a hundred million people*, brothers and strangers alike, a collective nightmare, a nightmare we had been imbibing all our lives and passing around to one another, feeding innocently to our newborns—that we are worthless, that we deserve no better than the filth we live in . . . If there is a Judgment Day, this was it. We rose from our graves, patted the dirt off each other, looked each other in the eye. An entire population crawling out of a mass grave to hold those who'd buried us accountable, and in doing so daring to imagine another reality. *It doesn't have to be like this*, my neighbor told me, and when I repeated this idea to my other neighbor, *It doesn't have to be like this*, I heard him pass it on in a voice that was louder than mine. We took heart from one another. As with every command from the natural world, the timing was right. All over the country, red-breasted birds appear at the first rain after the long summer, what we call, in Shobrakheit, the Date-Washing Rain. Every April, termites hatch like clockwork, conquering whole neighborhoods with their organization. In January of 2011, we, too, came out of the ground by the thousands, like a natural phenomenon. It was not a political coming-of-age, or even an ideological one. We didn't take to the streets out of anger, but out of pride. For some of us, it was the first time in our lives we believed in our own capacity for goodness or heroism. I was in the square every day, documenting what we were already calling revolution, and the world was all eyes. Cairo was flooded with foreigners—journalists, translators, activists, academics. It had never happened before that the global epicenter tipped in our direction.

Suddenly America was watching *us*. In its gaze we became a collective: demonstrative, intentional. We wanted to show them who we were. Each of us in the square had our work and felt it keenly. There were the organizers, the drummers, the journalists, lawyers, medics, poets, artists, those who distributed food and water, those who brought tents to share, those who warned us of spies and informers, and the informers themselves who failed to blend in. I had the digital camera then, and I sold CNN my frames for two thousand pounds apiece, close-ups taken on the ground and aerial shots from various balconies, all this before drones made it so much easier. I sold my work to the BBC, too, and to Reuters. I felt that my entire life had been a preparation for this exact purpose, that I was fulfilling my grandmother's prophecies, avenging the senselessness of her death and the teeth someone (but who?) had pried from her mouth, the cheapness of the burial, the wooden marker on her grave fading fast, instead of the marble plaque she deserved, carved and inked to resist the weather. Everyone in the street had a personal grievance. There was a woman we called Mama Batta, whose only son had been abducted by the secret police at age sixteen. When they found the body, his fingers and toes had been severed and sewn on again, the toes on the hands and the fingers on the feet. She carried his photo on a wooden sign. There were microbus drivers and mechanics, pharmacists, upholsterers, plumbers, farmers, shopkeepers, accountants, academics, all with photos of their loved ones too: this one dead from a curable disease, this one from suicide, this one in a building that collapsed. There was Uncle Sousou, whose kidney had been stolen on the desert road, and a landowner from Mansoura, who had had twenty acres of good farmland sequestered by the army without compensation. In 2011, we really believed we were birthing a new order, that everything would change and the corruption that had seeped through the veins of the nation, poisoning every organ, would be flushed out at last . . . Six years later, it's embarrassing to remember just how innocent we were—not naive so much as innocent. Those who were gunned down without even a crowbar in their hands to defend themselves we called martyrs and repeated their names and hung posters of their faces everywhere we could, determined that their bloodshed would not be in vain. We believed, we really believed that the revolution would succeed on the strength of our brotherhood, and the nobility of our cause. Had we been less occupied with documenting the losses, circulating names and dates, video footage, we might have noticed earlier that everything was not as it seemed. There was money pouring in from overseas, along with vested interests. We thought we were toppling a regime, but the whole world was involved. It seems so obvious now, but if you weren't there, you can't possibly judge. I can't tell you what it was like.

QUESTION: How many questions can you ask before you expose who you are?

———————————

I'm caught between my desire to understand and my desire to appear as though I already understand. In the mornings, the shop-keepers and doormen are all out on the street thrashing water on the gravel, making mud of the dust, so when I trail through on my way to work my hems are browned. What's that about? Do they imagine they're cleaning? There are manhole covers chained to dumpsters and dumpsters chained to lampposts. Who is stealing which, and what for? On every corner, a man sells corn, a man squats on the ground fanning corn bedded into the coals of a tin box, and yet I've never seen anyone either buying or eating corn. There are women balancing loads the size of washing machines on their heads, winding calmly through the traffic, arms by their sides. Everyone walks in the road instead of on the sidewalk. Fresh bread is bicycled through the traffic on enormous bakers' trays. There is a long pig-snort, a snore-sound they call *shakhra*, that people make when incredulous—the equivalent of an eye roll. There are ordinary things missing in the supermarket: baking soda, chocolate chips, tampons, fresh milk . . . There are goats in the road, chickens and rabbits and ducks in spindly wooden crates. If I keep my mouth closed, I can almost pass for a Cairene. People look me up and down, they talk to me in Arabic and I feel I've won something. When I start asking questions, they switch immediately to English, as though correcting themselves, putting us both in our places. Cairo is not what I expected, but the shock is one of scale rather than content. I expected traffic and poverty and pollution, but not like this. It's a city dialed up to its extreme. Sami and Reem had to teach me how to cross the road and live. They each held one of my hands and we practiced. If there are lines on the road, I've never seen them—just swarms of cars, each lunging forward wherever a foot of tarmac is visible, horns blaring, the drivers hanging their elbows out the windows, sweating, swearing at one another. Compared to New York, this is a real place where real things happen. Not microaggressions that are tweeted about, not theory; these are adult aggressions, bodily, bloodying. The beggars are missing arms or legs and come up to tap on the glass, show you their stumps, open their mouths to show you no tongue. They wipe the windshields with rags. Children, eight or nine years old, pull carts over potholes, look for plastic in the garbage piles or sell socks and balloons on the corniche. You buy a balloon and that child eats, or you don't buy a balloon. It's sensory overload with nowhere to hide. It's consequence. When I Skype my mother during rush hour, she keeps asking where I am, because it's so loud she can hardly hear me, but *I am inside, Mama, with all the doors and windows shut. Call again after eleven p.m. Maybe then you'll hear me.*

QUESTION: If this one cigarette was two cigarettes a year ago, where did the second cigarette go?

―――――――――――――――

When the foreigners left, it all went to shit. When it all went to shit, the foreigners left. The sequence hardly matters, the result was the same. They took their work and their money and their drugs with them when they left. Even the Egyptians who flooded back in from abroad in 2011, in hopes of rebuilding the country, have since given up and returned to wherever they came from. At some point after the Rabaa massacre of 2013, after the sugar crisis and the floating of the Egyptian pound last November, after it became clear that all the men who had disappeared from their beds at night for tweeting were not going to be released, the unthinkable happened: people began to long for the days of Hosni Mubarak. *He was a thief, but at least the economy was flourishing,* they began saying. *The wheel of production didn't stop once in his reign. He didn't lead us into any wars. He built bridges.* It's been six years since the revolution and the pound is worth a third of what it was worth in 2011, depreciating so fast that none of the shopkeepers put prices on their goods anymore. You have to hold up every can of ful individually, every pack of Cleopatra, and ask, *How much is this today?*

QUESTION: If one day all the other carpenters start calling you a queen, how many hammers will you need?

I first met the boy from Shobrakheit at Café Riche in downtown Cairo. I was there because I had nowhere else to go after work. On the street, my shaved head made me an easy target. Everyone had something to say. Women giggled. Men shouted from the backs of motorcycles and the interiors of cars. But in Café Riche with Sami and Reem, I felt semi-intelligible. They had Instagram references to understand the buzz cut, the one-inch coffin nails I came with, my crew socks with Nike slides. In fact, they didn't just understand me, they competed for my attention like spaniels, always yapping appreciatively about how *clean* I was. *Clean* being code for more than just money; a coveted un-Egyptianness, a combination of first world contact and old-world etiquette. Reem herself was clean because she was French-educated, lived in Garden City; Sami was clean because half-British by blood. Café Riche was clean because it had air-conditioning, a menu in English and French, exorbitant prices, waiters dressed in the jester-like costumes of Nubians; Umm Kulthum herself used to perform on its small outdoor stage. You can order a glass of wine with your meal but not shisha. All the tablecloths have the original Stella star on them and on the walls there are photographs of the celebrities who used to frequent the place. Café Riche is over a hundred years old and it is *clean*. The three of us were sitting around in its garish white lighting. They were teaching me how to play backgammon when the boy from Shobrakheit entered: freakishly tall, ducking to avoid a concussion on the door frame. He was dressed in suspenders, a frayed polka-dotted bow tie, and—most touchingly— black socks inside black schoolboy sandals. Sat beside me and twitched for the entire hour, jiggling his rounded knees, stretching his neck, cracking his knuckles in quick, unnatural succession.

I'd never seen such restlessness. Even his quiet voice was quickly quiet, the way flies and roaches are: atwitch. He scrunched a cigarette butt into his plate and immediately lit another, scrunched that, lit another. I watched his automatic fingers and saw with my bedroom eye the cigarette sizzling out, headfirst, against a nipple. I borrowed his spoon to eat the coffee grounds at the bottom of my Turkish cup. *Isn't it bitter?* he asked in a cool, pattering Arabic I could barely catch. *Is bitter bad?* I answered shyly. He asked me what I *played*, meaning what I *did*, then lifted the grimy analog camera hanging around his neck to indicate his own answer. In the months I knew him, I never saw evidence of his photography and believed him solely because he didn't try to shoot me, as they all do, didn't say the line they all say, preying on the conceit of women: *Your bones were made for a lens.* It was because he never asked that I eventually stripped and lay down on the kitchen tiles of my L-shaped apartment, commanding in my lilting, infantile Arabic: *Take me from above.*

QUESTION: If a girl misremembers the first time she saw you, can you ever truly fill her eyes?

I saw the American girl's ankles first. I recognized the foreignness in their brown angularity. Before I could arrange my body in response to this realization, the rest of her had descended from the ceiling, down the steps, into the basement stationery shop. Petite, expensive-looking clothes, and hair shaved close to the scalp like a sniper's. I was seated, blocking most of the narrow space, but she swept past (over) me, her flying silk dress licking my knees. She had me trapped on the floor, nowhere to go. Right behind her were the kids from Riche: Reem, the lesbian with the starched, ironed polo shirt; and Sami, sweating fatly, his rimless eyeglasses sliding down his nose. She stood looking at the leather notebooks, throwing words over her shoulder at them in a horrific English, while I sat, poor boy down on the tiles near her ankles, in the shop that was also underground. Vain, obviously vain. She left without buying anything. The same sweeping silk on my feet and knees before she floated up the stairs, ascended into the world. *This is the dress you were wearing in the stationery shop*, I would remind her on the day I finally peeled it off her body. Her answer: *What shop?* She had not seen me at all. Until now, she thinks we met for the first time two weeks later, at Café Riche, when she borrowed my spoon.

QUESTION: If a man's anger is lovelier than his loveliness, what kind of ending do you expect?

In Café Riche, Reem follows me with her technical eye. Reem irons her underwear. She threads her eyebrows using a ruler, will not bite into food that is multicolored or multitextured. She makes murals for a living and showed them to me on her phone: there were no curves, just lines everywhere and the intersections shaded like a building plan. *People pay for this?* I asked and Sami interrupted with his usual smirk: *They pay* very *well.* When we first met, Reem's entire right arm was in a cast that she scrubbed with a kitchen sponge twice a day to keep it gleaming. She was mildly concussed. When we met the second time, she did not remember me and was turned on all over again by the angles of my jaw (to Sami she whispered: *like Sawsan Badr*) and the bones in my fingers (*picture them fisting*). According to Sami, since her accident—she'd fallen from the scaffolding on a job—Reem is less inhibited and eats with her left hand like an infidel. *But you're left anyway, aren't you, Reemo?* Sami teased; *left* meaning loose, meaning sexed and liberal. Reem lowered her eyes as if in prayer. *I do the Lord's work.* She turned to me and flicked her tongue. *Who else do you know that eats so someone else can get full?* The boy from Shobrakheit smiled into his cigarette and Sami tooted, *Madame, this is a respectable establishment!* That day in Riche the four of us were sitting at the usual table at the front when a crowd of girls with bad makeup and tight hijabs giggled in. They were dressed in leggings under knee-length skirts, plaid dresses over turtlenecks, and other layered combinations that I was only beginning to realize were indicative of no money, and therefore no mobility, a hereness no one would forgive. The kinds of clothes worn by the kinds of people who would not be called *clean* by either Sami or Reem. Sami, who I had never seen actually address a customer before, rounded both

23

chins on the girls and asked them without rising from his seat, *Café or restaurant?* The girl at the front froze midstep and the others clashed into her, the whole group swaying forward and snapping back, before she said, *Sorry?* I saw her glance at the backgammon board on our table, unsure who we were supposed to be, what authority we had. Sami repeated loudly, *Are you looking for a café or a restaurant?* Beside me, the boy from Shobrakheit stopped twitching for the first time all night, the better to listen, it seemed. He picked his camera up off the table with one hand and his knuckles whitened around it. I pictured him bringing it down like a brick on Sami's snub nose. *Café*, one of the other girls said finally. *This is a restaurant*, Sami answered, and then he eyed them above the dimes of his spectacles until they left.

QUESTION: Why ask a question that has no answer unless you want someone's tongue in your hand?

That blubber-tub Sami was at it again. Every time I go to Riche he pulls a stunt like this—turns customers away at the door because they're too visibly broke. *Café or restaurant?* he asked, and whatever the girls had answered would have been the wrong answer. They were unwelcome. It boils my blood. I can't tell if he believes this classist dog shit or if the whole performance is a flex just for me, to degrade me or remind me that we are not the same even if it's *he* who owes *me* money. I would have stormed out if the American girl weren't also there witnessing the scene with an expression of confusion on her sharp face. She didn't seem to understand, and I waited for a chance to explain it to her. I went to the bathroom and finished off the red pills that are the only thing keeping me together right now. I must look it too. When I left home this morning, all the dealers on the street were coming up to me mumbling, *Want strawberries, boss? Want chemia?* Street names for Tramadol, and I must be shaking without realizing it, I must have a look already, if they are coming up to me in these numbers, in broad daylight. The American girl was watching me when I returned. As soon as I sat down, she lifted my spoon off my saucer and began to diddle with the coffee grounds at the base of her cup. Then, without ado, she put the head in her mouth. More than a pea for intimacy, this, I thought, was a gesture of solidarity. Later, when we were alone on the street, she asked me if Sami didn't want Muslims in Riche because his family was Coptic. Adorable. *They don't hate Muslims, they hate the poor,* I laughed. She was shocked and I was very pleased. Perhaps, had it not been for this moment, we would never have come to love each other. But it was the look on her face in the grim street light. I could see her multiplying that small injustice a hundred times over, calculating its true scale across a life span. She was from America, rich, obviously, but it seemed she could still be horrified by the wanton exercise of power, and this singled her out from the others. I felt somehow that she was on my side.

QUESTION: When is a confession of addiction not a foreshadowing?

At closing time, when Sami gets up to count the money in the cash register, the boy from Shobrakheit waits for Reem to leave Café Riche. Then, when she's gone, he invites me for a walk. *You can tell a photographer's skill by his grip*, he informs me excitedly. But his grip is unorthodox. He wraps his right hand around the camera from the front, fingers curling over the top as though it were a pull-up bar. Practices shooting but doesn't actually click. He lunges, crouches, kneels, holding positions for whole minutes with his eye on the plus sign, his pointer finger on the shutter he has not released in years. He says nothing steadies the hand like cocaine. During the revolution, everyone was itching and scratching anyway, lice being unavoidable. He says lice lived even in their mustaches and pubes. You could travel with your own tent on your back, but you could not control who came and slept once it was unfolded. He himself hardly slept. Back in 2011, a single line could keep him awake for three days. The drugs were passed out with the sandwiches and water and vinegar and yeast. Boys as young as twelve were emptying cigarettes in order to stuff them with warmed hashish, loose tobacco. Or else begging to lick the wrist someone else had snorted off. He says nothing makes for revolution like cocaine. He has been clean now for seventeen days. Every sneeze joggles the brain inside his skull, so he has learned to stop sneezing. Closes his nostrils with one hand and flutters his lips like a horse when he feels a sneeze coming. He has nerves growing straight out of his scalp. He cannot rub his fingers through his own hair, it hurts. His eyelashes hurt. He blinks violently. His bones hurt. His left leg, he complains, is full and wet with sand. Says he will shoot again one day and he needs to be ready. Carries the camera around his neck wherever he goes. Says he will never shoot again, laughing switches to English and shrugs out the words I translated for him myself just hours ago when he found out I was an English teacher: *Whatzza boint?*

QUESTION: Can a man and a woman fetishize each other in equal measure, or must one always be outdone by the other?

I tell the American girl with the shaved head that you either smoke, snort, or inject. Strict matter of preference, no more shame in one than in another, but there is a natural progression. Smoking is stupid slow. Also less economical. There is the frustration all the time over the fumes you do not catch in the lungs, the expensive drug diffusing visibly in the air. It is sentimental for most of us. Reminiscent of innocent, thrilled beginnings: protest, conspiracy, army tank graffiti, tear gas and tent sex, downtown house parties full of sweating journalists and mahraganat, the Italian orgies in Agouza. All the foreigners were here to fuck. I would step into rooms like a drop of oil in a glass of milk, like an open drain. The women immediately began to circle me. When they realized I spoke no English, no French, no German—when they realized I spoke only Arabic—it seemed to answer a question they had been asking since they arrived in Egypt, land of kohl-eyed pharaohs and fellahin. They wanted someone unpolluted by modernity—an illiterate, straight from the village, with rough hands and hair of black lambswool, sexual hang-ups inherited with bestial customs. They wanted me to loom above them, dark and merciless. They paid for everything and laughed when I would not take off my shirt or pants, but it pleased them even more to be naked while I was dressed, to be prone while I stood pounding between their white legs. These older women, who had not learned how to say *Thank you* or *Bless your hands for this meal* in Arabic, would beg me in monstrous accents, *Neekni, neekni*. Not once did I lower my head beneath waist-level to pleasure them. I even told them that in Shobrakheit we never kiss, to avoid having to bear their lips on mine. I took what I could from them and moved on. For many of us, once the sit-ins were over and the foreigners fled and the sex lost its variety, it became impossible to smoke. Snorting co-caine, you taste it through your nose and the bitterness will convince you—if you had any doubts left—that this budra is poison. The naked tongue shrivels in its bed, but snorting remains most practical in public. Anytime, anyplace, little attention needed. I once snorted off my wrist in the middle of a street in Zamalek; by the time passersby had swallowed their shock, I was powerfully gone. A needle in the neck, though . . . I take a needle in the neck or sometimes the back of the hand or occasionally—but not for many years now—the classic forearm. The vein knows before the skin is broken what is coming. I swear the vein begins to swell and thump like a cock, the heart already heroic before the tip enters. Once in, the force is immediate. I could jump off the 6th of October Bridge. I could wrestle an airplane to the ground. The first day I spoke to the American girl was also the first day I deprived myself of a needle in the neck. Coincidentally, no relation. Having made my decision the night before, I was terrified of being left alone in my shack with the peeling walls and roaches, the pain—a mushroom cloud of nuclear devastation—in slow motion behind my eyes. I went to Riche to see Sami about my money, but the American from the stationery shop was there too. She was the only one not smoking, sitting with her regal back straighter than a door while Sami and the lesbian blew smoke in her face. They were playing backgammon. She borrowed my spoon to eat the coffee grounds at the bottom of her cup, and we could all see from the peach-plump wetness of her lips how the skin of her other, lower lips would look. Her Arabic was cute, barely there. I could hear her crawling through the language, using expressions I hadn't heard since my own childhood. She handed me back the spoon and the metal head was sucked as clean as the tail. She was hairless, I believed, all over.

QUESTION: If the shoe doesn't fit, should you change the foot?

The day after I met the boy from Shobrakheit, I tried to ask Reem why Sami hadn't let those girls into Riche. *What girls?* she asked. *The ones that came in the other night. You remember, we were all sitting right here.* We were sitting right there, at the table by the door. *Oh, the girls with the hijabs,* she exclaimed, just as Sami returned from the kitchen. *What girls?* asked Sami. *The girls wearing skin-colored Carinas under their dresses.* Reem winked. *Oh, the girls wearing dresses over their jeans?* he asked. *The girls with Carinas under dresses, over stonewashed jeans. The ones in high-heeled clogs? The ones with Huawei phones!* It was a joke they were passing back and forth; they were laughing. I wanted to vomit. *What about them?* said Reem when she and Sami were done, but I felt sick. In New York this would have been my cue to leave. I know the rules. I know what is correct, when to attack and who to defend. Once on the A train coming home, I saw a hijabi woman get spit on by a drunk and I raised so much hell, the whole car turned with me. Someone called the cops, and three Knicks fans on their way to a game surrounded the spitter, who was by this point slurring expletives, getting violent. Someone was filming and the video went viral before I'd even seen it. It's how I got my Twitter handle, @spitonme, and became someone people recognized on the street and at clubs. But in Riche, I didn't leave. I just sat and drank Stellas with Sami and Reem until closing time, and then walked home, worried that people on the street could smell the beer on me. When I left New York initially, I had thought Cairo would mean a dry chapter in my life. I wasn't expecting to find alcohol here, but in Riche, everyone has a glass in their hand. There are bars all over the city. When I went to Reem's studio, where she makes high-end stencil art for a living, she had all her empty liquor bottles displayed on a window-sill in a ray of sunshine. Later, at two separate house parties that she dragged me to with designs of seducing me, I noticed similar empty bottles arranged like trophies in the living rooms of first a filmmaker and then a journalist at Reuters, both well into their thirties. They treated it as a point of pride, even a form of activism, to drink despite so much flagrant religiosity everywhere else. Am I convinced by this? I don't know. In New York, alcohol isn't radical, does not set you against the grain or expose you to hatred the way wearing a hijab does or praying on the grass in Central Park, so it's disorienting now to be in a city where every Friday, mats are rolled out onto the street and businesses close up so the men can pray under the sun. Are those that don't participate, those who drink and sport tattoos, men with earrings, girls with shaved heads, discriminated against? Sure, we're outnumbered, but are we *persecuted*? Or is it the hijabis who are not allowed in "clean" restaurants and hotel swimming pools (as I learned from one of my students' essays) the ones I should stand up and defend? I am outside of my context, confused about where the margins and the pressure points are. Who has the power? Where is the center? I haven't seen a woman's knees since I got here, and no one has seen my knees either. There is Quran playing everywhere, and people drag God's name into every conversation. Every time I get into a cab, I am given a sermon by the driver about the wrongness of women looking like men, and why don't I cover up my head, seeing as I don't have hair anyway? But when I leave the car, having paid less than a dollar for a half-hour ride, I'm confused about my right to offense, just as I'm confused about drinking as an act of resistance. There is something entitled about it. Yes, there is something rich.

QUESTION: Have I gone blind because of the dark, or is it dark because I've gone blind?

I text the American with the shaved head. She does not answer. I text for days and she does not answer: the vanity of this woman. Meanwhile my body avenges itself. Six years of budra in my bloodstream and now all the pain I have not been feeling is slamming into me, compounded like, *You dog, what is yours will always come for you.* In the rooftop shack where I have been living for six years, I pace around naked, too uncomfortable to sit or dress. Every stitch on my back chafes me individually. When I eventually collapse onto the bed, I dream of Magdy, though I have never seen him. No one sees Magdy. He doesn't answer unknown numbers. A dealer's phone is worth its weight in heroin. I once saw a different dealer sell his SIM card for two hundred thousand pounds, back when that was a filthy number. But Magdy will never sell his phone. He'll live on a few loyals for the rest of his life. I dream of Magdy's voice, his effeminate, cream-white *allo*, fuller than a question. In the dream I ask for more budra than I could ever afford. I hear myself say, *Five—no, ten—I mean twelve. Twelve grams.* And Magdy breathes on the line like my father does in Shobrakheit, breathing things he'll never say. He breathes for minutes while I plead, *Magdy? I'm good for it, Magdy. I'm good for it. I need twelve grams tonight.* I pull fists of leaves out of both pockets. I pull hairs from my head for payment, a dirty clown-ribbon ten meters long comes out of my throat, and I'm gagging. *Good for it!* I wake up drowning in my own bed, the sheets heavy with sweat, swaddling me. I kick until I fall off my mattress and the concrete greets me like a shore. I roll on the ground until the pain subsides, then I text the American: *Photography is a gorgeous corpse turning on the first night in its bed of soil. Photography is a shawl caught on the finger of a gnarled, eternal olive tree. Photography is not about victory; victory is viler, baser than the loll of a child's head on that child's own chest.*

QUESTION: Is romance just a father who never carried you to bed carrying you, at last, to bed?

The boy from Shobrakheit began to text me relentlessly. I wasn't encouraging, but leaving him on read—which would be so communicative to any New Yorker—he didn't register as rejection. Or, possibly, he understood but did not consider rejection an obstacle. Every day I woke up to verses of poetry (likely his own), whimsical invitations, compliments, videos on YouTube, until, in a small way, I began to look forward to them. He sent me origami tutorials, clips from experimental German films of the sixties and seventies, bhangra playlists, Palestinian newspaper coverage of World War I from a digital archive I'd never heard of, and then, from the same year, scanned diary pages of an Armenian in Alexandria—a schoolgirl describing the boys she admired from church . . . I was surprised that someone like him could have such eclectic tastes, that he could be historically inclined and access a larger world through the cracked screen of his outdated phone. I couldn't help but wonder if he'd cobbled together this collection just for me, to prove he could. The first night we walked around downtown together, his voice had struck me as street—sweaty, full of scrap iron. But then he texted in an Arabic that was formal, even classical. I said to Reem, who was always smoking somewhere nearby when I got these messages, that I couldn't tell if I was being courted by an Azhar sheikh or a news reporter. Reem tried to ask what I meant, looking hurt and longing in that way she did when we were alone. She was in love with me. Her own texts consisted entirely of memes. I ruffled her hair. She flattened it again. Arabic: this language that had only ever existed for me in kitchens and bedrooms, baby talk, breakfast chatter, Eid mornings at the gym-cum-mosque (before my father converted to astrology), goodnight kisses after *Kalila wa Dimna*, or fever-talk when I was feverish at age five. Now, twenty years later, I realize I have never been loved by a man the way my father once loved me. The boy from Shobrakheit hot-wires an intimacy just by sounding like him. He wishes me not a *good morning*, but a *childlike morning* or a *morning of flowers*. He texts, *I hope your day will be like the birds. I hope your night will be like the childhood of trees. Don't be sad, my moon. I have a remembering of the lives I didn't live.* His texts also consist of theoretical food offerings, and in them I hear how the women in his family have loved him. *Here, have peanuts and buffalo milk,* he texts me. *Have gateaux, black tea with fresh mint. Come, eat pickled lemons from my hand. Have tomatoes with cumin. Are you happy? I am trying to please you with the little I have. Here, have grapes. Have a chocolate croissant.*

QUESTION: What if male arousal is only a gasp misplaced in the body?

When we met again, it was at the tail end of a heat wave, during which the poor and elderly, those who couldn't afford or didn't believe in air-conditioning, expired all over Cairo. I had twenty pounds in my pocket, so we sat at my ahwa under the bridge, where they charge me humane prices. The American wore a sheer négligée, floor-length but essentially bedroom, with gold earrings that oozed off her lobes like honey and a martial expression on her face. I've never seen such long eyes or such primeval bones. She looked like she had walked right out of the museum and I told her so. *You are pharaonic.* Every single eye at the ahwa was on us. A woman who exposes her hair in a city where most women cover their hair is already considered attractive—in the neutral sense of the word, meaning she will *attract* attention. But a woman who neither covers her hair nor exposes her hair because the hair itself is not there . . . A woman who, of her own volition, shows the skin of her brain to the public . . . The children of the bridge began to call one another until a small group of them had gathered, talking loudly about the man who was a princess and wasn't his a pretty dress and whether he would give them a pound. The beggar women selling tissues and peanuts did not come near us, probably thinking she was diseased—a young thing with her head shaved—but the men . . . The men were so shocked, their dicks stood up. They peeled up the silk of her negligee with their eyes. They parted her legs, cupped her scalp in their palms, and breathed steam out of their nostrils like horses. Every shisha hose was coiled translucent in their hands; they sucked and puffed in her direction. She began to tell me of her life as best she could. She told me her father fancied himself a dental prophet and her mother was across the ocean exercising herself to death. They were going through a divorce.

She was alone in this city, which explained some things. She was Egyptian enough to wax her arms but American enough to shave her head. She was Egyptian enough to sit at the ahwa under the bridge but American enough to think a silk nightie was appropriate wear at the ahwa under the bridge. She uncrossed her legs when she heard the athan, but then kept them wide at the knees like a truck driver. When we got up to leave, the giggling children pushed forward their bravest, who shouted in his cheap for-tourist English, *How are yewww?* She smiled in her own wannabe-baladi Arabic, *Tamam yakhouya*, then handed over a fifty-pound note for him and his friends. I cringed. They ran away before anyone could stop them, but I'm glad they did and I wish she'd given them even more of her money. It was in moments like this that she reminded me of the Germans and Italians I used to sleep with, who were so predictable with their sympathies in the months after the revolution. We'd be approaching a barefoot child doing his homework on the sidewalk and I just knew they would start fumbling with their purses. I just knew they would pull out an egregious sum, squat beside the kid, ask where his shoes were and his mother, take a picture of him without permission. They thought it made them look conscientious instead of guilty and voyeuristic. I always let these women empty their pockets without commenting, since there was something retributive about the exchange, a kind of tourist tax. And now with the American girl I catch myself doing the same thing: just leaning back, watching the scene play out, not tempted to intervene at all . . .

QUESTION: If you are competing to lose, what do you win if you win?

_____

He told me he was from a village, Shobrakheit. He told me a New Yorker and a Cairene have more in common than a Cairene and a man from Shobrakheit, but he would not tell me what the commonalities were. Instead he asked if I had ever ridden a microbus, and I was forced to say no. *What about a tuktuk?* Another no. And then I remembered that when we'd stopped at the kiosk for cigarettes, he had bought singles. I looked and seemed to see him for the first time: the hems of his pants were frayed, strings dangled from his vest like lines of saliva, yet he wore a perky bow tie. He wore black leather sandals with socks, but one of the soles was loose, flapping like a bottom lip when he walked. I didn't know then: every night before bed he washes his feet and socks in the sink, wrings the blackness out of both. Hangs the socks on the bathroom door handle to dry for the morning. Only pair he has. He washes his socks every night but he has never brushed his teeth with toothpaste or shampooed his hair. Does not own deodorant. If he showed a little more ideology, he could be considered woke—some kind of minimalist, an ecofreak. How to say *consumerism* in Arabic? How to say *toxins, microplastics, mutagenics, fair trade, ethical sourcing*? But the boy from Shobrakheit doesn't give a reason for not shampooing his hair—just says he doesn't like to. What's a hipster without intentionality? Old-fashioned and proud and poor. Also, Egyptian. More than anything, what binds people here to one another here is the pointless struggle for quality of life. I'm learning slowly that having money and the option to leave frays any claim I have to this place. It turns out that to be *clean* in Egypt is just to be free of Egypt, to exercise the choice to stay or go elsewhere, which most of the population cannot do. The boy from Shobrakheit will die never having crossed a border. He is so tall that when we walk around downtown at night, his hair catches on the butchers' hooks, which are black-tipped, yanking, the blood beneath them never dry. He took me to get liver sandwiches from a cart on the street, but not the popular cart. *The popular cart is a pound more expensive per sandwich, which is robbery*, he said. We sat on the sidewalk to eat, and I knew he had chosen the ground because I had chosen the crème slip-dress, which would catch the dust like a wet tongue. *But I take the metro all the time*, I said, remembering that I had ridden it once when I first arrived and that it had cost as little as a pound, as little as six cents American. We test each other.

QUESTION: Is a country boy trading country stories for city stories from a city girl getting ripped off?

I was born and raised in Shobrakheit, Beheira, a small farming village of mulberry trees and bicycles, kite wars, stacks of rice-grass piled three stories high, ninety kilometers from Alexandria. It is known only for its Napoleonic relevance, as site of the 1798 battle between the French army and the Mamluk cavalry, and for black magic. Apart from the rare pilgrim historian, the only visitors to Shobrakheit are Arabs, who come from as far as Yemen and Morocco. Depending on how much money they are willing to spend, one of two sheikhs in Shobrakheit will lift works off their loved ones, or else rid them of jinn-riders. My own cousin had a work on her from age six to age eight. When it was removed, she vomited a mango she had eaten two years earlier. The work may be hidden in a piece of food that is consumed or in the womb of a tree or in the belly of a fish in the Mediterranean. A Saudi woman once came to a sheikh in Shobrakheit crying, *I went all the way on foot from Riyadh to Mecca, and when I got to the Kaaba I couldn't see it.* To which the sheikh famously replied, *Woman, you put a work in the mouth of a corpse buried twenty kilometers from the nearest village—of course when you went to the Kaaba you couldn't see it.* In Shobrakheit, before the internet, our only contact with the larger world was through newspapers and television. As children, after watching *Titanic* at the village cinema, we built a boat from enormous blocks of Styrofoam we had stolen from the only store that sold imported household appliances like kettles and washing machines. We tied them together with rope—also stolen—and floated the whole pathetic contraption in the Nile. After watching Mel Gibson revolt against the execution of his lover, we built forts out of stacks of ricegrass and inside them played war with slingshots or else fucked the poor girls from the other side of the river.

In 2011, when I returned from Cairo for the first and only time, my father came to meet me out by the pigeon tower, so he could enter the village with his arm around my shoulders—his son, the revolutionary with the city hair that stuck up on all sides like a sunflower. I stayed for one week and, that whole week, dizzied around the house that had never homed me, like a trapped moth. People from all over the village came to us for news of Cairo, and my father did not leave my side, so proud was his breathing.

QUESTION: How far can you run from home before you have to face what your father has done?

Why do I keep seeing him everywhere? My slim-faced, long-boned father, with an accent in both his languages, with the papyrus framed on the wall of his waiting room and the oud charming his patients over the speaker system. My father, who went through the tedious legal work of reverting his name from Freddy to Fouad, after realizing the marketability of the Orient in the Manhattan alternative health industry. In 2004 he suddenly became a fad. *The first holistic dentist in New York*, his business card exclaimed, along with other such desirables as *oil pulling, bloodletting, authentic North African remedies for Western dental catastrophes, 9,000 years of medical experience!* I resent him because I recognize him. This desperation to refashion ourselves into the most pleasing form makes fools of us both. We're pliable and capricious, shed our skin at the slightest threat, and ultimately stick out everywhere we go. We were both more convincing Egyptians in New York than we'd ever be on this side of the Atlantic. There I had enough Arabic to flirt with the Halal Guys and the Yemenis at my deli. At school, identity was simple: my name etched in hieroglyphics on a silver cartouche at my throat. I could say, *Back home, we do it like this, pat our bread flat and round*, never having patted bread flat or otherwise. But here I keep saying I'm Egyptian and no one believes me. I'm the other kind of other, someone come from abroad who could just as easily return there. In Arabic, I keep using the wrong verb tenses or mixing up the feminine and the masculine, and they pick me out immediately. It helps to stay quiet. I keep nodding, pretending I understand and then frantically googling phrases late at night, but not everything is googleable. I tried to tell a taxi driver I wanted to get off on the west side of Zamalek, and it was like he'd never heard of west. No one uses the cardinal points for directions.

The Dokki side? he asked and I wasn't sure, couldn't say. The maps are all wrong. Where the roads are numbered (rarely), they are not ordered consecutively, and when they are named, no one uses those names. The landmarks are arbitrary—a discontinued post office, a banana-seller. The bridges are referred to by dates. *I'll take the 26th of July to Zamalek and then you point where you want to get off,* the driver says politely. It's as though the city were deliberately designed to resist comprehension and to discipline those who left for daring to return. You have either lived here and you know, or you never have and never will.

QUESTION: Is a father who won't speak up for you the same as a father who can't speak at all?

―――――――――

My father is a mute. He plays with rubber tires for a living and disappoints everyone around him. A mechanic. When I was seven, he tried to marry the neighbor's fifteen-year-old daughter, a girl so immature she used to throw clothespins at the frogs from her window when they were too loud at night. He did not succeed, but Mother still left the house for three years in protest. Although he was mute, not deaf, my mother had long adopted gesture as her primary language. When upset with him, she might remove all the buttons from his good shirt or offer only radishes for dinner. While they were in this stalemate about the potential second wife, I was deposited in the care of my grandmother, a dough-bodied woman who was infatuated by paper. She had learned from a book, before YouTube made it easy, how to fold paper the Japanese way, and had a whole room in her two-room house by the river for her collection of paper cranes and lotuses. When I came to her at the age of seven, she made space for me in her narrow bed, and that was how we lived. It was more generosity than I had ever known. We lived like royalty, eating when we wanted, whatever we wanted—I grew four inches in my first year, breakfasting on cake from flour she had ground herself—sleeping rarely, swimming often in moonlit rivers. We danced American in the room of cranes, my arm around her waist. Most people, when they learn where I am from, expect that I had a backbreaking childhood, that I grew up drinking a glass of steaming ghee every morning, swallowing garlic cloves whole, and heading out to plow the fields. The truth is, people everywhere need to do more than just eat. In Shobrakheit, there are lawyers and electricians, musicians, tailors, knife-sharpeners, teachers, drivers, plumbers, doctors, carpenters, blacksmiths, architects, painters . . . There is a woman in

Shobrakheit who makes buttons. There is a man who hand-paints signs and wedding invitations. My grandmother dreamed I would make films like Youssef Chahine and that one day they would be screened in the village cinema. When I turned nine, she sold her wedding gold to buy me my first camera and wove me a leather band with which to hang it around my neck. After three years of this pleasure, word reached my mother that I wanted to eat peas. My grandmother was on her way to the market to buy them. It was summer, and Mother, who was not affected by three years of separation, was suddenly moved to illness because her son wanted to eat peas. She came back to the house my father still lived in and cooked so many pots of peas—she who used to count peas, she who still splits tangerines—that my father called a sheikh to dis-possess her, and still I would not go home.

QUESTION: If a city is actively trying to kill you, should you take it personally?

Four days a week I Uber to the British Council in Agouza, where I spend all day conjugating verbs on a whiteboard, enunciating the names of colors and the months of the year, as clearly as I can, in English. None of the students want to be there. In the morning, I teach teenagers, and in the evening, adults, men in suits who try very hard to get my phone number. I am the only Egyptian teacher at the center, so I'm the only one who can recognize them outside of their broken English, the only one who can restore their manhood to its full height. After hours of struggling to pronounce foreign triple-consonants, tripping repeatedly over words like *February* and *present progressive*, they can switch to Arabic when our class is done and have their egos instantly restored. They flirt with me and horse around with each other, competing for my benefit. I let them because it helps; language acquisition is such humbling work. I tell my students as much when I first meet them and make it a point to speak some Arabic so they can hear my own clumsiness. Though I joined the center only six weeks ago, my classes are quickly becoming the most popular and I am bombarded daily by students in the hall begging to be let in from the wait list. *Miss*, they say in English, though some are old enough to have birthed me. Then they whisper conspiratorially in Arabic, *We both know the IELTS is a scam, and no one here is qualified to teach— but I need to get at least a five. Please! You can't squeeze me into your class?* The other teachers dislike me; they sense I am fraternizing with the students against them. Sometimes we all go out for drinks after work and then the dislike is palpable. They feel threatened. Only one or two of them—men, obviously—make an effort to be nice to me. When I come home at the end of the day, I am filthy and exhausted—but amazingly filthy. Filthy in ways that seem magical, given the route I have taken since leaving the shower that same morning. There is dust caught in the hairs of my eyebrows and upper lip. It lines the inside of my bra. When I blow my nose at the sink, the mucus in the porcelain bowl is black. No matter how short I cut my nails, they acquire black sickle-tips. I spend twice as much time bathing to feel clean for half as long. At the ahwa under the bridge, I complain to the boy from Shobrakheit about the dust and he smiles enigmatically, tells me a moth wing is in fact only dust petrified into a fine sheet. As a child, he used to collect them. He used to catch dragonflies, too, and leash them to a half-pound coin with hair he plucked from his mother's scalp. He used to shoot birds off the telephone wires at dawn and leave them on his mother's pillow, inches from her cheek. He used to suck on his grandmother's breasts, long after his mother weaned him off her own with the bitter cactus meat she rubbed on them. I am careful not to react to this information. *But surely there was no milk*, I say. *There was no milk*, he confirms, *but it was a gesture of nurture*. I say, *And you remember this? You were old enough to remember?* He says, *How could I forget?*

QUESTION: If your first love does not live forever, how do you forgive yourself?

Then when I turned sixteen, Mother sold the house by the river that my grandmother and I were living in. No one in Shobrakheit knows how she did it. The house was in my name. Grandmother put it in my name to keep it safe from my mother, who still found a way to sell it to an upholsterer, a piece of a dog's religion, this criminal known to lend his wife to his own brothers when he was drunk. She sold it and didn't tell us. One morning we were evicted like whores by a line of sniggering policemen, my grandmother wailing in her flowered house-galabeya while they carried out our refrigerator, our bed, our table with the food still on it, while they stepped on her collection of paper cranes with their field-boots. She had been married for only a year before her husband died. She was a proud and loyal wife, and afterward lived independently for forty years, despite the family pressuring her to remarry. She lived with my grandfather's memory alone, and it was enough. Then, at age fifty-eight, she was forced to move in with her daughter, and the humiliation killed her long before the dinners could, long before the oven. She and I took the downstairs and shared a bed as we had always done, but it was not the same. We ate bread and beans, no cake, and these weasel-portions of fruit. My grandmother stopped dancing, she stopped folding paper the Japanese way. When she killed herself, I washed her body with my hands as she had washed mine for half my life. I remember her body as though it had been my own. She was almost boneless, her meat so soft, almost edible, then the long, sagging breasts. Because of the burns, her skin was rippled like river water. Her mouth was empty, full of dark red holes, the remaining teeth having been pried out by someone, probably to sell to the dentist across the river. Boiled and de-rooted, they could have been planted as crowns in the mouths of other patients. After all these years, it's this thought keeping me up at night, keeping me as far as possible from home: that her molars could be shining still behind the lips of someone living. Her molars. Her thin incisors, like grains of basmati. When my grandmother crawled into the oven—when she. And lay there cooking without a sound. The rest of us sat at the table, Father breathing, Mother fanning an even number of arugula leaves on each of our plates. We almost started eating but the smell caught us just in time. I was the one to find her. At the burial, I carried the plywood casket on my shoulders through the streets of Shobrakheit and within six months had lost a third of my body weight.

QUESTION: If the men make animal sounds in your direction, which of you should get the bone?

_____

I've been shitting liquid since I landed in Cairo two months ago and no one can tell me why. When I complain to Sami he says without skipping a beat, *So stop eating dog meat off the street.* I forgot I had told him about the liver sandwiches I get a few times a week with the boy from Shobrakheit. *What do you expect?* he snaps. *Street food isn't clean.* So I stop eating from the liver carts, but the diarrhea continues. Reem says it is probably the produce. *Are you peeling everything? You have to peel everything.* So I become one of those people who peel even peaches and tomatoes, but it doesn't help. *Bottled water, even if you're cooking with it, even if you're just boiling pasta or making tea,* says Sherry over the phone. *The tap water is sewage, dear, don't trust it.* I cut out everything I can short of starving myself, but nothing is working. I'm losing weight, coughing up lead-colored phlegm, asking myself ten times a day: *Why did I come here?* My mother is sobbing in all her spinning classes halfway across the world as my father, a holistic dentist—how to say this in Arabic?—divorces her from our summer home in the Poconos. Meanwhile, in Cairo, I'm buying shawarma for a three-legged dog sniffing in a garbage heap, all the men laughing at me. It's exhausting—the levels of dysfunction, the sheer effort it takes to complete even the simplest tasks: crossing the street, buying fruit, changing the gas cylinder in the stove . . . Everything is more circuitous than it needs to be. To pay my internet bill every month I have to go in person to a Vodafone outlet, where I am handed a number by a man who is hired to stand beside an automated machine and press the buttons for customers who apparently can't press the buttons themselves. I wait for about forty-five minutes until one of the employees is free and I can pay by credit card. Often the machine is broken or the system is down. *When will it be back up?* Could be an hour, could be a day. Neither the Vodafone app nor the website allows me to pay remotely. *Why even have a website?* I ask. *You can pay your bill over the phone,* a clerk tells me. As it turns out, I cannot. And this is just the internet. There is an assault course for every other bill and errand. There is the garbage, there are the crowds. There is the harassment on the street, which excited me when I first arrived, my mind delighting in theorizing ahead of my body: *The Egyptian catcall is a form of social engagement, an interpellation of womanhood, increasing the potentiality of every public space, so refreshing after Manhattan, where no one looked you in the eye!* But now I'm completely worn-out. Reem keeps trying to convince me to go to Dahab with her, to get out of the city for some sun and sea, but I doubt I'd survive the seven-hour drive. If Café Riche weren't a five-minute walk from my apartment, I wouldn't make it even that far. Some days I leave the apartment with the intention of heading to Garden City for a film screening or over the bridge to Zamalek, and I make it two blocks down the street before turning around and going straight home. Even when I wear the swathing, swaddling fabrics my mother packed for me, I can't blend in. I'm recognized as an outsider and keep getting asked by complete strangers where I'm from. To my answer *Here,* I'm smiled at magnanimously, as in *Of course you are.*

QUESTION: If your father once put his penis in your mother, how do you get even?

News of pornographic films first reached the boys of Shobrakheit in '99. I was eleven. Two villages over, in a garage surrounded by fields of sugarcane, a sheet was hung on a wall. A projector was duct-taped to the ceiling, and the only light for miles around was its light. There was a front door and, at the back, near a man cooking mehalabeya, there was a hole covered with a plastic tarp for customers to escape through in case of a police raid. The plastic chairs were set in rows. The cook had the sharp, veined, wicked arms of a widower with four sons and no daughters. He made watery rice pudding and mehalabeya in tin bowls. Ten piasters a bowl, and this was expensive. At midnight, we all gathered at the pigeon tower. We were aged between eight and twelve, the older ones with coats over their pajamas, and the younger ones, hopping from foot to foot, without. We walked an hour along the bank, and the frogs of the bank punctuated our steps, jumping as high as our waists, belching ego. When the first boy cut into the field, the rest of us broke into a run. We skipped, and one of us began to sing, *If we stop dreaming we die*, and another sang, *Come to me, boy, what's it to me, boy*, our pockets chinking with a month's saving and stealing. The entry fee was two pounds, given to the cook's youngest son, a hilarious, bucktoothed boy with the hopeful name Elmohtady-Bellah. When we filed in we were ignored entirely. We sat on the floor at the front of the room with our necks snapped back like feeding chicks, mouths open. Stunned. We didn't speak or swallow for two hours while women, tall white women, had things done to them by men and then by animals. They wore no clothes on their skin, had no fat on their muscle, so they seemed doubly naked—even the breath was being smacked out of them. They were panting and whimpering, begging for it to stop. By the end of the screening, four of our boys were crying. We walked back to Shobrakheit with the dawn just breaking behind the fields. When we entered the village we found every father from every household waiting by the pigeon tower to drag us by the hair.

QUESTION: What if female arousal is just the belief that you will not die at this man's hands?

———————————

Every few days we meet, but always outdoors, on a street corner or at an ahwa. He avoids interiors. There's an itchy what-next-ness about him that is most acute in confined spaces, even those that are familiar, like Riche or the stationery shop on Sherif Street. He automatically ducks through any doorway he enters, expecting that his height will not have been anticipated. Then he folds his lankiness into the nearest chair and shifts around, waiting for a bell to ring so he can bolt out the door. One day I tried taking him to an exhibit of photography at the Townhouse Gallery, thinking he would like it. To get there, we walked down Mahmoud Bassiouny, where I live, then turned onto Champollion. It was warm. We were holding hands. When a schoolgirl passed by us with an oiled braid down to her waist, he said abruptly, as if inspired, *Show me a picture of you with hair.* I snapped, *Show me a picture of you without,* and he laughed so hard we had to stop walking so he wouldn't trip on any of the mechanics' feet. These were strewn up and down Champollion, twitching as though their owners were being gently chewed by the vehicles they were under. I couldn't help but smile. This preoccupation of men in Cairo with my grooming made being outdoors as uncomfortable for me as being indoors was for him. But I knew he'd meant no harm. He couldn't understand what it was like in my body, on the street, without him. In New York I used to shave my head in the bathroom mirror once a month. I tried to keep this up in Cairo with the electric razor I'd brought with me (the stupid device whining shrilly since the voltage here is too high), but every month I noticed myself delaying the shave and then going a little higher on the clipper guard size so my hair got longer and longer—I was losing my nerve. I prefer the clean look of a number one, but increasingly it wasn't worth the commentary. When it was that short, strangers on the street were always calling out *salamtek* because they thought I had cancer. A beggar once even refused my change, saying, *You need it more than I do.* When my hair was a little longer, I got called other things: *whore-boy, sissy-boy, faggot, biscuit, bicycle-rider* . . . Even with my hair at its longest, I got misgendered if I was wearing pants. To avoid this, I made a point to wear my biggest earrings and dresses, a little lipstick when I went out, and always headphones to drown out the barrage. Only the boy from Shobrakheit didn't notice the subtle changes in my appearance. We had been talking for two months and he seemed to only just realize, when he saw the schoolgirl, that I, too, must once have had hair long enough to braid. This is what he was like, what I liked about him: a transparency that seemed at times a failure of imagination but at other times a form of respect. He didn't think too hard about where I had come from or where I was going, how different we were from each other. He just assumed a warmth of feeling. That I had left him on read for weeks was not personal, for example. That he had wanted to see my hair wasn't a rebuke for its lack. He was just curious, communicating a whim, nothing more. You could see right through to the bottom of him. When we got to Townhouse he hesitated before entering. There were many people standing outside smoking, dressed as they would be in Brooklyn or Berlin. From inside, we could hear jazz and the hum of a large crowd in conversation. I felt him straighten his camera around his neck, as though it might explain to whoever was in there why someone like him had come. The gallery was an enormous, repurposed warehouse in a humble neighborhood full of tradesmen, and I thought this, of all places, would be comfortable for him. We walked in. The lights were bright. It was opening night and there were garçons milling through the crowd with plates of hors d'oeuvres. He turned around and walked right back out of the gallery. I decided to take him home.

QUESTION: If a girl freely admits she isn't a virgin, can you believe her about the price of milk?

August. We were arguing about balconies. The American paid two hundred times my rent and claimed it was worth it for the balconies. I'd never been alone with her indoors before. She said, *From all four of my balconies you can see a canopy of bat-infested trees and at sunset they all get to screaming.* I said, *Show me.* And she did. Ashamed of her body. When I took off her brassiere, she covered her nipples; when I took off her under-wear, she covered her cunt; when I took her hands off her cunt, she covered her eyes and stood there shaking her head like a little girl afraid of a ghost. I didn't believe her for a second. The more fucking a girl has done, the shyer she pretends to be. It is a rule. But I will extract their names from her in time. She has the slimmest calves I have ever seen, I know at least ten men in America have circled them with their fingers and thumbs. She has the cleanest ears I have ever seen; I put my tongue in them. She has the deadliest sideburns. Men in Cairo don't have an appreciation for sideburns. It is a strictly country aesthetic to see them smudge against the ear, so close to the neck. We were naked in a soft light and my hunger climbed, it shouted through my shivering, like a bitch being drowned in the river. I insisted because she wanted me to. She said *no* but she meant *yes*, wanted to be pushed over the lip of the glass but did not want to be seen wanting it—this sudden coyness, so uncharac-teristic, perhaps the only Egyptian thing about her. She said *no*, no again, more faintly this time, and my hair caught in her eye-lashes, clung to the wet sides of her lips. This hideous pleasure at a woman's softness after months of only roaches and needles. She touched me as though petting flowers, and I held her scalp in both hands. Yes, she meant *yes*, so I gently pushed us both over the lip. We fell into each other, heaving with dry sobs. Afterward, I asked her what she was thinking as she drifted off to sleep. She sighed dreamily with the whole of both lungs like a woman in the arms of a man she loves. Then I swear I heard her say: *Pomegranate seeds.*

QUESTION: Can you be good together if you don't look good together?

It was only when he came home with me that I realized I had never been alone with him before and that there was something unnatural about doing it now. When we appeared at the entrance of my building, the doorman stopped what he was doing—clipping his toenails, one foot on the hood of a parked car—to look the boy from Shobrakheit up and down. I had never seen the doorman behave rudely toward anyone. His face was openly contemptuous. *That elevator only takes two people at a time*, he said loudly but not to me. There was a sign on the elevator door saying as much. *We're two people*, I countered as I got in with the boy from Shobrakheit and slammed the skeletal metal door, trapping the doorman on the other side with both his feet now on the ground. We went up with a shudder and the next time I came down in the elevator, I came down thankfully alone.

QUESTION: Does furniture recognize—or does it make—a stranger in the house?

So this is how she lives. The first night when I went up to see her balconies, I didn't see them. I couldn't see anything but her small face and shiver-body. Only when she left the next day for work was I able to examine the place at leisure. Her apartment is in one of the older buildings in downtown Cairo, a corner unit on the seventh floor with high ceilings and classical trimmings on all the balustrades. But the inside is insane, furnished with what she refers to as *pieces*: kilims handwoven by Faiyumi bedouins; bookshelves that smell of wintered linseed oil; hardbacks in English and German, which, when opened, reveal ribbons and leaves pressed into their hearts; an enormous steel water filter with a piece of coal inside it; an antique French canapé; orchids that she feeds with an eyedropper and hides in a room I am not allowed to smoke in; a stool with three red legs in a slab of unfinished concrete; a gurgling air purifier; a phonograph; a seamstress's bust draped in pearls . . . The tables and chairs are all arranged as though for a portrait, at their best angles, with haughty upturned chins and arched foot soles. She leaves the shutters open day and night to display them to the world. The only mess she allows herself is littering the floor with her clothes (the silk dress she wore a week ago is still a puddle in the corner of the bedroom), but otherwise the space is intentional, sensorial. She tells me the apartment was rented furnished from a distant relative, an academic who lives most of the year in Berlin. But even if this is true, enough of it is her own. She belongs to this apartment as much as I don't. It reminds me of the places the foreigners used to stay in, in 2011, which were always equally perverse. You'd walk in and be confronted immediately with the feeling that all the furniture was living in denial of its geographic circumstance, that the human who had done the arrangements was afraid of the city outside her windows. But in the American girl's apartment, she is perfectly comfortable and I am the one slinking around the rooms like a thief, unsure where to sit or what to do. She comes and goes "to work," and I stay in this apartment that could be anywhere in the world—if it weren't for the balconies and me in it.

QUESTION: Can home be passed from one body to the next, like a secret whispered in the ear?

He tells me that in Shobrakheit they never call a woman by her name in the street, least of all a mother. He tells me it's no one's business outside the family. *If I want to call out to my cousin, I use her husband's name. If I want to call out to my mother, I use my own name and she looks up.* I ask him how he used to call out to his grandmother and he says, *I wouldn't need to call, I'd be by her side.* Is this why he doesn't like it when I go out alone? I always assumed he was jealous, but could it be protectiveness instead? When we are on the street, he moves naturally between my body and the traffic. He plucks my purse off my outer shoulder and rehangs it on my inner shoulder, where motorcyclists whizzing past cannot snatch it. Around every corner he expects a criminal, but everything is always fine. We are wizards together: a bald woman and a long-haired man in fantastic dragging clothes. All we need is a leashed monkey and some sort of instrument. We walk the streets and everyone ogles us. If he disappears into a store for a minute, everyone is whistling, hollering, hissing, *He tricked you, honey, and now he's wearing your hair! Is your cunt as clean? I could like that.* He comes back out and hasn't heard any of this, but he's seething as though he had. Expects it somehow. Stomps his sandaled socks and walks like a tantrum. Later, he points out scenes from the revolution as if proving his machismo to me, threading pearls around my neck. *Qazaz—that was the Brotherhood's, everyone bearded in there, Quran playing day and night. The kids wiped it out with molotovs. Now look, no beards and they have music playing like a normal restaurant. This store sold gas masks, that one gunpowder. There is a woman on the third floor of that building who used to throw bottles of vinegar and bags of yeast to us from her balcony, both being antidotes to tear gas. Pepsi also works well. This is where Sobhy heard a bullet with his ear—it went in the left and out the right. That is the apartment Al Jazeera used to film the square from. Aren't you lucky to be here with me? Who else could tell you these things? No one else will tell you these things.* He was right. Who else could get me up to speed? After so many lifetimes of peaceful eating, a nation overturns the dinner table; there is the darling outrage, a newfound entitlement, hope, yes, hope—and then betrayal. Disillusionment. That sheepishness, afterward, at having been caught believing. For every Egyptian of my generation, this will be the greatest political event of their lives, the drama they return to and repeat to their children and to their children's children to explain the world they are born into. I missed it entirely. Watched the revolution on television from the comfort of my home on the Upper West Side, a French bulldog on my lap. How convenient, then, when all is said and done, to arrive in the riskless aftermath, claiming, *Me too, I'm one of you.* I'm too late returning and he knows it. As long as we are outside, on the streets in this city that he owns, he leverages his knowledge against me. When we come home he is less powerful, less instructive. But why do I say *home* as though he lived here? Does he? He came up one night, slipped my dress over my head, and never left. We've been playing house for the last two weeks. Except that I'm both father and mother, bringing home the meat and also cooking it while he waits for me with his cheek in his hand. Do I mind? It's nice to crash into his chest when he opens the front door. He hears the elevator and comes to meet me before I can finish turning the key in the lock. I used to shower and go out after work, to Riche or the bars in Zamalek, but now we stay in more and more. It's getting cooler. We run hot water over our bodies and he soaps the day off my skin, kisses the top of my scalp, we make love everywhere. I have more than enough food to share. We eat by the light of a Siwan salt lamp. He asked once if there was a spare key and I said I would make him a copy, but I don't.

QUESTION: If a fly rubs its hands delightedly all over your excrement, is it a compliment or an offense?

She is nicest to me when feeling vulnerable herself. Occasionally she returns from work with her eye makeup smudged, looking fraught, frayed at the edges. And then I can count on her to cry at the slightest permission. I love when she cries, how the kohl streaks down like two braids on either side of her mouth, that genital mouth of hers. Then I can comfort her, make her laugh. I know just what to do. Other times she looks at me with an appetite that is romantic but wrong: Curious, consumptive . . . anthropological? As though she were peering at a moth pinned to a corkboard, shivering, still very much alive. As though she were laying it on her warm tongue, letting it dissolve there. It's her American showing: rolling into my village in a military tank, tossing at my mother's feet three-quarters of an apple she has only peeled with her teeth. Then I get so wicked I make up things just for her. Fantastic things that it tickles me to imagine her repeating to her gullible friends on the phone, reporting live from the front, like some kind of authority. I tell her my grandmother used to cut my hair once a month with a knife she had licked to sweeten the blade. I tell her my grandmother used to save the hair she had cut, tie it around a stone, and toss it into the Nile so birds would not build their nests with it. I tell her that if a bird builds a nest with even one of your hairs, you get a migraine. You can't just discard willynilly things that once belonged to you, even if you've outgrown them. You have to be careful. *Some things*, I say my grandmother used to say, *are holy.*

QUESTION: If a man and a woman call lovemaking by different names, can they still?

He tells me, *Some things are holy.* Hair trimmings, for example, the inheritance of orphans, the first cigarette after a fasting day, a widow's loyalty to her husband in the grave . . . He looked so serious, I couldn't help but laugh. *Why shouldn't a widow remarry and have some fun while she's still alive?* He swore and stood up, knocking his plastic chair back onto the road. But he didn't leave. He just stood there and looked around, as though he didn't know what came next, had forgotten his lines. Then he lit a cigarette, righted the chair, and sat down again. *A man wants to know who will close his eyelids when he dies*, he explained, though that was not my question. I snorted because I wanted to know what came next in this scene where he loses his temper and towers above me. *So if his eyes are closed, she should close hers too?* I goaded as he continued to smoke and didn't answer me. He is both childishly romantic and a hater of women. But even as I goaded him then, even as I remember the goading now, I grow tender about it. As though he were some snarling puppy I'd found run-over in the road and assumed responsibility for. Yes, he could be misogynist, but he was also valiant and sentimental, poetic, young-hearted, a weirdo in his way. Years after the pornographic screening in the garage, after he learned where his father hides the dirty VHS tapes (rolled in a blanket among the winter quilts) and how to watch and rewind them as though he had not watched or rewound them, his grandmother made him promise never to open a girl. That is, the taking of virginity: opening the way a sealed envelope is slit laterally with a butter knife. By then, the boy from Shobrakheit had opened a girl already. He was twelve. She was twelve, and all the cousins regularly squirted each other down with hoses in the field or played hide-and-seek with the lights off, a variation they called the Dark Room. It began innocently, a touch like any other: her fingers around his ankle, pulling him out from under the bed. But after the game was over, they continued to seek each other, find excuses to be alone together, in the fields or at home. They touched each other during the years and years of their schooling, under his mother's roof or hers, with no one suspecting. He opened her, and when she married the butcher's son from down the road, she pushed a string of raw goat meat inside her so her husband could open her again. Afterward, when she tried to keep coming to her cousin for sex, the boy from Shobrakheit threatened to light her hair on fire. No love between them. He was not even jealous of the husband, only could not stand to double-dip. Now he walks touching the heads of street children, looking like a prophet, a flat-footed caveman. You can see the dream of water in his wet-lashed doe eyes. His brows. His hair so black it is closer to white than it is to brown, shoulder-length, curling wetly, smelling of biscuits. The jaw of a man women want to please. He referred to what we did together either in his heartbreaking English as *se-kess*, or else in formal Arabic as *a bodily engagement*, or else in slang as *making one*. He closes his eyes during. After, he loves to be the little spoon.

QUESTION: If you're waiting for the other shoe to drop, have you not thrown it yourself?

There is always the sense that this is a trial period. She loves me but she isn't sure. I've been clean for three months now, but it hasn't gotten any easier to pretend I'm well. I keep snapping under the stress, flaring at her; then she retreats outdoors, spends longer hours at work, avoids me for a few days as though recalibrating. At night, while she sleeps, I lie awake and fight off fantasies of Magdy. Some days the only thing saving me from calling him and going down to score, ruining everything I've been suffering toward, is this apartment. I don't have a key, so when she leaves in the morning for work, I'm effectively trapped. If I took the elevator down, I'd be on the street. Would the doorman even let me back up? When she got home, would she let me in? I can't explain even to myself how I know what I know: that we must avoid at all costs enacting this question. Our relationship is fragile, sustained by habits we intuited from the beginning and now adhere to. I spend most of the day waiting for her to come home, the hissing, heaving Schindler elevator announcing her, seconds before she steps onto the landing. She may be the one with a key in her hand, but it is me looking through the keyhole, me opening the door before she reaches it. She's never home without me. I'm never out without her. Every Friday we take a walk on the corniche, then breakfast somewhere so the cleaning lady can do the apartment without ever finding out a man lives there. If we run into the doorman, she reaches instinctively for my hand. We might go down to the ahwa for a midnight coffee or to the butcher for some meat, but leaving together implies returning together; she doesn't invite me up, because she doesn't have to. There's no pause for deliberation, no real option presented. We just go up together automatically. We do what we have done a dozen times before, delaying hand in hand for as long as we can the decisive moment: when it is me on the other side of the door, asking to be let in.

QUESTION: Can a building designed to humiliate ever stop humiliating?

The boy from Shobrakheit cannot boil water. He says he's had a rough life and I'll give him that. He's been getting it in the neck for years. He showed me the mosque on Abd El-Khalik Tharwat, where he slept when he had nowhere to go, and his body bears scars in places that should not have seen sharpness. So, fine, it's been rough. But even so. The boy can't boil water or heat bread on the eye of the stove. Leaves the milk out of the fridge. Tries to cut an apple in the night and I wake up to blood spattered on the kitchen floor, seeds everywhere. There is all the evidence of a past tended by a woman's hands—he's at least as spoiled as he is damaged, I mean. When I feed him an ear of bread with tahini and molasses, he takes it naturally between the teeth. Kisses my fingertips one by one, and then the knuckles. We sleep and make love and eat and make love and sleep. We live like a married couple dreaming domestic dreams, until he wakes me up. One night I came home several hours late, having gotten drinks with some of the teachers at the British Council. He didn't say anything but followed me into the kitchen, where he noticed, seemingly for the first time, the door leading to a hidden staircase beside the stove. He stared at it for ten seconds before calmly lifting a glass and throwing it against the wall, demanding, *How can you live in a building that used to have a servants' staircase? Don't you know anything? Don't you have principles?* It was the first time I saw him get nasty and I recognized immediately that it was not about me, not about the classist architecture of my building. Rather, it had all become too much somehow. I held his gaze and said nothing until he left the kitchen, then I picked up the glass shards and swept carefully, thinking, *He senses that his usefulness is depleting.* Ever since he showed me how to buy vegetables from Bab El-Louk, I no longer need him to buy them with me, and I come home already laden with plastic bags. I've become familiar with the butcher he introduced me to, who keeps his meat in fridges instead of hanging outside to be smoked by car exhaust and wormed by flies. I've learned which pharmacists are actually licensed and where to buy bread that is fresh no matter what time of day or night you arrive. We no longer explore downtown Cairo together so he can point out to me his memories. Four days a week, I go to the British Council, and when I come home, he's there waiting, already at a boiling point. When he threw the glass against the wall, I didn't react. I puttered about making dinner while he watched YouTube videos in the next room and filled the apartment with clouds of smoke. He didn't offer to help, didn't even glance up as I trailed back and forth with pots and plates, glasses of orange juice I'd hand-squeezed that morning. I would never tolerate this dynamic in New York, but here, somehow, it is harder to speak to. He is punishing me for something, and I am letting him. He is weaponizing all his losses against me, and I am wanting the abuse, or, at the very least, accepting it as mine. After years of claiming Arabness as an excuse for what I am—hairy, hard-boned and dirt-skinned, sensual, impulsive, superstitious, nostalgic, full of body-shame and estrangement—I feel I'm earning it at last. The hazing is belated but confusingly sweet. I have a guilt, and the boy from Shobrakheit has an anger. In his sleep, he taps his pointer and middle fingers to his lips. Dreaming of a cigarette. Sometimes he rubs the thumb-side of his hand along his philtrum and sniffs. Tonight he made me a watch by biting gently down on the skin of my wrist and drawing numbers around the imprint of his teeth with a pen. It is a small apology, I know. It will be three o'clock all night. *I made you a watch*, he says.

QUESTION: Who does a nude belong to—the one who takes it or the one taken?

Every few weeks she asks me why I don't do photography anymore, and I have to bite back my temper. If you have documented a revolution, how can you bring yourself to capture anything else on those same streets where your brothers stained the asphalt with their lives? I used to sell a single frame to the foreign news channels for two thousand pounds back when two thousand pounds was a filthy number. There were a few of us then—Sayyed, Khorshed, Mezo, and others—but after Morsi was dragged by the beard and we had to watch yet another dictator co-opt the movement, it became difficult to keep believing in photography as arsenal. It didn't matter that we were back in the square all over again, recording every moment with the same people that had come out two years earlier, the same tents and sandwiches. In fact, many of the photographs we prided ourselves on taking for posterity's sake, as archival testaments to the martyrs and believers, the heroes of our time, ended up being used against them. Since al-Sisi came into power, thousands of those who accidentally put him there disappeared overnight, many of them identified through our footage. There are more political prisoners in Tora Prison today than passed through it in the last four decades; men, all of them young, from poor backgrounds, who have no friends in high places to get them out, since we were their friends and look where we are now . . . Today, only those without a conscience are still working. Some photographers know how to sell their own, they play the grant game—funding from the Goethe-Institut, scholarships from the Swedes, filters and hashtags, peddling themselves on Instagram—or else they become common fixers, pimps, smearing our nudes all over the wet magazines overseas. I haven't raised my camera to street level in years, despite carrying its deadweight everywhere I go. I could show her my work from 2011 on CNN, but I don't. Her question is a capitalistic reproach. She wants to know where I get or don't get my money, how I could ever afford a cocaine addiction. She teaches English to adult men at the British Council, but what do I do? She wants to see for herself what I do. The night she stepped out of her clothes and sat down, I thought she wanted to have sex on the kitchen floor. But then she stretched out, her watery breasts slipping to the sides of her rib cage like raw eggs, her stomach hollowing to make a bowl. With her scalp on the ceramic tiles, she closed her eyes and said, *Shoot me*. It was dark. We had just come from outside and the camera was hanging around my neck. I looped it up over my head and, without taking my shoes or coat off, shot her. She lay perfectly still. Her skin pimpled all over from the cold floor. I nudged her legs apart with my heel, the better to see what she wanted to show me. I got her again and again, kneeling down as close as I could, and each time the metallic sound of the shutter was louder than before and more mercenary. I shot her face too. Then roughly flipped her over to capture her back because that was what she wanted. I understood that this was a kind of fetish, that she was no different from the Germans and Italians who wanted me to talk dirty to them in Arabic, insult them, call them whores and dogs. They wanted to be mistreated in language they didn't understand. I kicked her over onto her stomach, using the toe of my shoe like a spade, and she lay facedown, shaking for a long time, but not from cold or fear.

QUESTION: Is it racist to believe that being sexist makes you more Egyptian?

The kitchen is the only room in this apartment without a balcony attached to it, and he seems to feel safer there because of it. There isn't even a window. It is the darkest room, day or night, closest to the hollow inner column of the building, where the staircase winds around a steampunk-style elevator—just an iron cage with an accordion door and all the dubious gears and pulleys visible. Every other room in the apartment is porous to the street, especially with the shutters thrown open like I have them. Light ghosts in from the backs of billboards. The honks of cars accent the rooms along with the brittle smacks of backgammon chips, the dry cleaner's soap operas, the calls of fruit vendors and junk collectors, old men barking from minarets . . . And we are also leaking our private lives out, adding our commotion to that of the neighborhood. If the smell of onion frying at the kushari place next door reaches us, so the smells of our lovemaking must reach them, the clinks of our silverware, the starry smash of a glass against a wall, voices raised. All the windows are open, so if anything went too loudly wrong, someone might come knocking. It's become clear to me that Egyptians are meddlesome, full of Good Samaritans who love to hear a woman scream so they can swoop to her rescue. I remember at the ahwa when I made the widow comment, how the boy from Shobrakheit stood up in front of everyone and then sat down again, shaking with impotence. What could he do with everyone watching? Am I safer with him on the street than in my own home? Am I safer on the balcony than in the windowless kitchen? Would he have thrown a glass at me in any other room?

QUESTION: Is it arrogant to grieve the loss of what you never had?

In the city they sell a gram of budra for nineteen hundred pounds, but I can still get it for twelve hundred from Magdy because I am that deep in his phone, have been loyal to him for that long. If you venture into the desert, the bedouins will sell you that same gram for 900 pounds, but the trip will milk years off you. Over the sink, the American washes her face with brown sugar and I remember my mother sweeping salt grains off the kitchen table into her hand with the sharp edge of a store flyer, so as not to waste them. Before the mirror, the American smooths and curls her sideburns with a waxy-headed toothbrush, something I've never seen anyone do. When she takes off her clothes, she leaves them dead on the floor. By the end of the weekend, the whole apartment is littered with twisted, tortured pants and shot dresses, brassieres fainting over door handles and the arms of chairs . . . Yesterday I realized it is because she was brought up with a Mexican maid who picked up after her in America. As she's leaving in the morning for work, I wave at her from the balcony like a proper housewife, a fresh bride who soaks her skin all day in buffalo milk to soften it for kneading. I spend the hours she's gone watching YouTube videos, reading Nietzsche in translation. She comes back at sundown, starved, beat, defeated by the world. Some nights I hold her in my arms as she drifts off to sleep. Other nights I can't even do that. She's probably never met an addict in her life . . . How to explain to this woman the exhaustion I feel after a long day of not moving? Not caving, not scoring, not shooting? When she strokes my cheek against the direction of hair growth, I shiver uncontrollably. My body is not finished with me yet. It continues to avenge itself for all those years of substance dependence. But because I don't explain all this, she doesn't understand why my pulse is so faint I can't find it. Instead of a left leg I have a sand-filled sack. If I stand up too quick everything goes dark. In the dark—is my skin still on me? I can't see otherwise. My nerves wriggle in the air and—pain. Does she know the meaning of that word? Pain, it's pain. I am careful to simplify my language when I talk to her, but not too much. Her range is odd, at times jejune and grandmotherly, at others formal, obsolete. She uses words like *naughtiness* and *tummy* but *beg pardon* when she means to say *what*. When startled she invokes God in the language of the Quran. When she curls into my chest, I want to wax poetic, unburden myself of every secret, but I know she will not be able to keep up. Misspells everything like a kindergartener when she texts me. I am careful to define unfamiliar words. *Let me tell you a secret,* I text her as her body sleeps against mine, her nose in my chest. *I can no longer be like the fountain. The fountain is a structure that spurts water, usually in a roundabout or public plaza. It squirts water from several mouths. I feel that love should flow freely, as water does from fountains. Let me ask you: Is it possible to contemplate a thing—any thing at all—without sadness?*

QUESTION: How long does a newborn listen before it utters its first word?

I woke up to find he had tried to explain a fountain to me, as though I didn't know the word. He was sleeping with the phone still clutched in his right hand. I texted back on my way to the British Council, saying, *Nice sadness but don't feed it. Its tummy is holey, so it's always hungry. If you feed it, it will befriend you and will return every night to beg like a street dog. A dog is a four-legged animal with fur and paws that coughs when it wants to be heard. People put a string around its neck and walk ahead of it on the street. It is considered impure by some religious schools of thought.*

QUESTION: If your lover lives in a building grand enough to have a servants' staircase, how long before she sends you down it?

You are condescending toward the street dog.

QUESTION: How many fingers and toes will you sever before you're small enough for a man to possess?

If I had been able to speak to you in English, you would not have thought I was condescending toward the street dog. I can see it happening almost before it happens—all the ways I will be misunderstood. I am trying to express myself with the vocabulary I have in Arabic. I am stupid in this Arabic, a blubbering toddler in his arms, defenselessly drooling all over his chest. Meanwhile he peers down at me from his height, his muscled tongue clicking, spitting. There is nowhere to hide. When I try to reply, I choke on the gutturals like gulp after gulp of sea-warm sperm. The boy from Shobrakheit leans over me and his hair pricks my open eyes. His hairs are so curly they shed from his head already coiled into a ball, no strand to speak of. I find these all over the bed and in the corners of rooms, like the souls of insects who've died on their backs. He doesn't say, *You can't see your friends anymore.* But after a full day of teaching, if I am late returning or if I return only to leave him again for the bars in Zamalek or Café Riche, I know he will be waiting, counting every minute I am gone, chewing them like seeds. We fight often. I go out less and less, have not seen Sami or Reem in weeks. My world is getting smaller. He doesn't say, *Stay with me,* or *Hurry back,* but there is always a fight when I come home. *Do you realize all your friends are straight guys or gay girls?* he asks, and I snap, *What are you trying to say?* He lights a cigarette and ignores me. *What are you trying to say?* I shout and he begins to get up slowly like an old man, leaning on his own thigh, squinting, panting, baring his gums. *Are you calling me a slut?* I shout. In the living room, he straightens to his full height. He picks up the red-legged side table, swings it as though to fell a tree. I duck. There is the sound of metal thwacking wall: solid, intentional. Then a gape of silence. He says, *Look what you made me do.*

QUESTION: Which is more frightening—to wake up with injuries or a weapon in your hand?

It's not my fault I don't speak English. It's not my fault my father fixes tires instead of teeth. He didn't leave this country when he could. He stayed here with the crooks and quacks, dentists whose instruments ring with tetanus, typhoid, hepatitis . . . men without a conscience who will rob calcium even from a corpse's mouth. We buried my grandmother without a single tooth in her mouth—do you understand what I'm saying to you? Do you hear me? Her lips were folded over her gums, and the rest of her . . . I can't even. My father is a mother-cunt, too, but he is not a lucky mother-cunt in America, he is not even a lucky mother-cunt in Cairo. He's on his knees day and night, patching rubber in Shobrakheit because Egyptians like your father are in America. Because. It's because, you understand? Who do you think is funding this regime? Why do you think we're still in this shit? Six, nearly seven years later and— you think it's an accident I have two hundred pounds to my name right now? Yeah, what you spent today on Vodafone credit, what you spent yesterday on imported shampoo because you hate this country you chose to find yourself . . . I have nothing to offer you. What can I offer you? I bring you bundles of mint leaves because I can't afford the sugar apples you eat with both hands and drip all over your chin. Do you know how it feels, knowing I can't even buy sugar apples for a woman I love? Do you know what I do when you are at work speaking English with the other English teachers? The blond ones from London and Canada? Willeem or Willam, who light up your phone at night, who you're probably fucking because you're a ten-pound whore? Why are you crying? Why are—don't act like that. Don't cower like I'm about to hurt you. You know I'd sooner hurt myself than hurt you. I almost jumped off your beloved balcony yesterday. Don't you know you're the only good thing I have? That you hold spoons by the middle the way my grandmother used to? That in the hours you're not here, I don't get out of bed? Have no reason to eat a meal or change my shirt. If your father were here, I'd ask for your hand, I'd . . . What am I supposed to do to be enough for you? I don't speak English, because I went to public school in nowhere, Shobrakheit. Do you know what a public school is like in Shobrakheit? She doesn't know. She can't imagine. When I was still in elementary, my grandmother used to come at noon with a bag of sweets to encourage me to stay the full day. *They're not teaching anyway,* I'd tell her, and she'd say, *But maybe tomorrow they will be.*

QUESTION: If the beast is already in your house, does that make the wilderness safer?

He cried. After he swung the table at my head, he crumpled to the floor in what my mother has been calling child's pose ever since she took up yoga. He cried and I heard through the gasps, *I'm not well. Can't you see I'm not well?* The first day he walked into Café Riche, I didn't notice the holes in his pants or the threads slobbering off him, the lipping sandals. He came in huge, with a stiff, dark-shouldered masculinity and whimsical bow tie. Then he refused to meet anywhere that wasn't the ahwa under the bridge. I hated it there: just plastic pool tables and chairs on the street, the asphalt muddied beneath us, weasels slipping between our ankles, the noise of traffic unbearable. We drank coffee in shot glasses that still bore the lip-prints of previous drinkers. Then he rolled his sleeves up and I saw the scabs and scars up and down his arms, the twitching. He told me from the beginning he was an addict, but now I believe him. Now he is calling me a whore ten different ways. And now he is crying on my living room floor in what my mother calls child's pose. I look again: Boy defeated. Boy from Shobrakheit with nothing and no one but me. He says he would have married me—how on earth could he have married me? I try to imagine him swishing kombucha around a glass with my father in what is now his permanent home in the Poconos, and I snort; he howls harder at my feet. He gets smaller and smaller, howling, *What's funny? What's funny? Are you laughing at me?* The boy has never left this country, never will. He is in child's pose, wetting my floor, offering me imaginary peaches and chocolate croissants. Why is this pity I feel so frightening?

QUESTION: If an Egyptian cannot speak English, who is telling his story?

We fall asleep in each other's arms. We watch a film together and fall asleep in our outdoor clothes, in each other's arms, her scratchy head beneath my chin. The grief numbs us both. I find myself measuring for the first time how far America is from Cairo, let alone Shobrakheit. How to bridge this ocean? How to explain all I left behind to get even this far? The mulberry trees, the microbus and train. I dream of Magdy and my grandmother together in bed. He is on his back on the phone, taking orders, making good money; meanwhile she rides him like an unbroken horse, her house-galabeya hoisted up around her waist. When we were still two, my grandmother and I, living in the house on the river, she'd come out of the bathroom after bathing, thighs blubbering against each other and her smell preceding her down the hall. I'd pinch her where the meat of her belly folded over the meat of her thighs and she'd scream giggles. How to explain the devotion between us? At some point in every country family, the son becomes the father and the grandson a husband. For the last ten years of her life, I was the only male to see her hair, to hear her thighs clap against each other. When we moved in with my parents, I knew she would die. Every night fruits were quartered at the table. Father breathing over them, Mother measuring. How could she not die? She who used to fold paper, she who danced with me in the room of cranes. I could not even close her eyelids—they were fused together from the heat. And how she kissed mine every night . . . Her lips were sagged in, as though sucked down her throat by too ravenous a heart, her gums soft as mud banks, tops and bottoms sinking into each other. She was the first of all losses. When she climbed into the stove—when she. And the smell of her—the wrong smell of her. Dinner. In the house forever in the village. I untangle myself from her arms. Go out onto the balcony with the bat-infested trees beneath it and make the call.

QUESTION: If you understand why a hound is snapping at you, have you already pardoned him the meat from your leg?

I'm not stupid. I know the signs of an abuser, check them off a list as they flash by my window like 100km, 80km, 40km, 10km—we're headed straight for collision. How to say *passive-aggressive* in Arabic? *Guilt trip? Victim complex?* How to say *emotional blackmail?* What is unforgivable in English, in Arabic has no name I know. *You are trying to make me feel bad*, I say like a small hiccuping girl with sand in her eyes. *You are no longer safeness*, I tell him. *I miss my*self. He hugs me and I let him. On my laptop, we watch a young Mahmoud Yassin stalk Faten Hamama until he possesses her in the 1971 classic *The Thin Thread*. When he calls the film a romance, I realize very clearly what he wants from me, and also that next time this boy from Shobrakheit won't swing and miss. What once was peculiar in him, charming, even, is now terrorizing beyond words. It's not his fault. He doesn't speak English. It's not his fault he has no work. There is no work to be had; all night long the downtown sidewalks and doorways are haunted by whip-thin men who abuse pharmaceuticals, make animal sounds at passing women. *What do you want me to do?* he asks. *You want me to serve coffee at the ahwa under the bridge? You want me to sell peanuts and tissue paper or earphones at Ramses? This country has milked the tits off me. You weren't here, you didn't live through 2011, when we thought—we really thought . . . And now look. Is this what we fought for? Is this*—fuck. *You blame me for not separating plastic from metal in the garbage heaps? You know how much a kilo of plastic goes for?* I don't know how much a kilo of plastic goes for and he doesn't ask how much the British Council pays me. He doesn't have to. We hide our finances from each other but the numbers chafe between our bodies while we sleep, so that we wake up full of static, agitated, zapping everything we touch. I did not even apply for work at the

British Council. My mother made a call and arranged it before I even arrived in Cairo. She was even embarrassed to make the call, to tell her former classmate Sherry that her own daughter, a Columbia University graduate, wanted to teach English for less money than she pays the maid in New York. My monthly salary is roughly what a dog-walker in Manhattan makes in a week, but here it is enough for several months' rent. More money than he'll ever have in one go, but what can I do? Who is to blame?

QUESTION: How long can you hate yourself before everyone else hates you too?

I swear this isn't who I am. I'm not a violent person, but there is a violence that moves through you like a live current when you hate what someone has made you become. I feel estranged from myself the longer I am with her, made criminal solely because she is afraid, made pathetic because she pities me—a poor boy though I never was. Of course, the end was always coming, but I never imagined it would be me putting myself on the other side of the door, deciding enough is enough. Before I leave, I text the American from two feet away, where her body sleeps, warming the room with her breath, the laptop still open beside her with the film we were watching: *Addicts, like grandchildren, do not fill their hours. They pull the hours apart, entertain themselves by melting the hours into new shapes: a ring, a gray braid down a bare back. Occasionally the hours fight back with passion so the addicts and grandchildren are transformed into the bleeding of a nostril or ear. Bleeding means the wasting of time, but it can also mean the loss of blood, as in: I bled from the nostrils. The nostrils are the two openings of the nose.*

QUESTION: If an ending is as wrong as you expected, were you wrong or were you . . . ?

In the morning, the boy from Shobrakheit is not there. Gone, his cigarettes, his dear schoolboy sandals, my laptop gone, my mother's pearls. I check every room twice and under the bed. The side table is still on its side in the corner, the red legs having left red streaks on the wall. All the breath I have been holding for weeks comes back to my lungs when I empty the ashtray, lock the door. He has spared me the messy job of getting rid of him. I close the shutters on all my balconies, blocking out the smudged, unclean sky, and remember how he predicted this weather. When we first met in June, he told me that every November the rice farmers burn their grasses on the outskirts of the city and that for weeks it would blacken what should be blue. This is the first day I notice, or perhaps the first day they begin the burning. In the shadowed apartment, I deep-clean all the fabrics, scrub and sweep the floors. I rearrange all the furniture. It is three days before I finally text him back to say: *The nostrils are the two holes of the nose, and the word nose suggests both curiosity and snobbiness, and what is meant by snobby is the rice remaining on a plate at the end of a meal, and what is meant by plate is one of a pair of kidneys (usually the right) in the body of a woman.*

PART TWO

ONE SHOT and I am like a god: headless, high as a cloud. I see two government informers[1] on a nearby street corner making their waddling way in my direction, and I rumble under my breath, *Come at me, boys.* There is one more gram in my underwear but I am too tall to be suspect. I am strong, straight-backed in the ocher air, the roiling, hard-boiled atmosphere. I shoot finger guns at the sky. *Look at this, boys, how I impregnate the clouds with lightning.* The balding informer, who is a step ahead of the other, opens his palm and looks up. Water is falling from the sky in drops the size of human tears. After vegetating underground for so long, a stranger to my body, I feel the need to flex a little, to stretch and be daring. Even my inner monologue is actively recovering its reach, catching flittering, long-forgotten classical couplets, country saws, profanity. Living with a woman whose Arabic is stunted, I never noticed how much I was mirroring her: walking on my knees so as to seem shorter. Now it is so good to be back to my full height. Somewhere above me, sheets of corrugated tin clash. The lights of the world flash on and off. The informers shrink from me in fear—what is *the state* before a man?—slouching one behind the other, protecting their faces with a pudgy hand, a sopping newspaper. They hide their long-nailed little fingers from me;[2] later they will go home to beat the fat off their wives. I pocket a couple gooseberries from a fruit stand and no one stops me. I high-five all the posters of al-Sisi, then wag my middle finger at his constipated expression, the ends of his lips turned down like horse tails. I hop onto the steps of a public bus and ride one foot on, one foot off, all the way downtown.

---

1. Despite their efforts to blend in, government informers in Egypt are always recognizable by their state-mandated painter's mustaches.
2. Just as the fullness and lining of a woman's lips advertise the fatness or pucker of her vulva, in Cairo, the little finger is considered a good indication of the length of a man's flaccid penis. Men with insecurities, sexual or otherwise, are prone to lengthening the nail of that finger to give the illusion of being well endowed.

I Skyped my mother at last. After months of evasion, claiming the internet was too scratchy for video, then waking up regularly to multiple voice notes on WhatsApp, each with varying degrees of abandonment hysteria, I called her one morning out of the blue. It was the middle of the night in New York and she was awake with a bottle of Bordeaux, hugging it to her chest like a loaf of good bread, no evidence anywhere of a glass. I expected tears, the usual guilting performance directed at Chichi in the corner of the room—*Look, it's my daughter, who left, just like her sister, just like my husband left, and now she calls, can you believe it, Chichi, now, after everything, she remembers her own goddamn mother*—but my mother answered quietly instead, smiling, none of that. *It's good to see your face*, she said. As it turns out, this is much more effective. I put my face down on the table, not the red-legged one that a man swung at my head just three weeks ago, but a blond dining table in the same room where I had sat so many times, peeling tangerines with my leg extended beneath the wood, my curled foot in his two-handed lap. My shoulders heaved. Mother nodded. It was one of those ugly cries you don't want to see in the small, square representation of yourself at the bottom of the screen, the one you will allow only in front of pets and mothers, never males of any relation. When the boy from Shobrakheit left me, I celebrated his absence, closed all the shutters and watched eight seasons straight of *RuPaul's Drag Race*. I rearranged all the furniture and read Don DeLillo aloud to the houseplants. I ate sweating cheese slices and strips of pastrami straight off the Styrofoam and didn't go to work for days. On-screen, Mother was still nodding when I looked up. I stopped gulping just long enough to ask, *How's Chichi?* before dissolving again at the familiarity of the living room halfway across the world. Somewhere off-screen Chichi began to howl, having heard her name in my voice. My mother's face, my mother's body on the leather tuxedo couch, in the silk robe that pointed at the nipples, with the wine she loves, with the enormous shaggy fiddle-leaf fig in the background . . . I said, *Mama, every morning the men splash water on the street outside their shops.*[3] *Why do they do it? Do they imagine they're cleaning? Why is everyone wearing parkas and beanies in eighty-degree weather? Mama, why do so many men grow their pinky nails to such witchy lengths? Do you have answers to any of these questions?* My mother said, *When are you coming home?*

---

3. The practice of splashing water outside of shops and homes is a cultural remnant of the Mamluk period in Egypt, during which streets would often become flooded at prayer times from worshippers performing their ablutions in outdoor fountains. Over time, puddles became the sign of a pious neighborhood, and to impress arriving guests, residents began splashing water on the streets outside their homes.

IT REQUIRES ELEVATION. There is only one point, from the middle of the 6th of October Bridge, where trees do not conceal her apartment entirely and visibility is possible. The easiest way to get there is to climb up the bridge from Abdel Moneim Riad Square, keeping your back to the river. There is no sidewalk, because this part of the bridge passes over only roads. Why would anyone on two feet want to go up there? The motorcyclists bully me for trying since I am in their lane. My left hip is brushed by passing side-mirrors and handlebars. When I get to the spot, I turn and lean against the railing to make myself narrower. I count the floors, seven up or five down, squinting to see through the drizzle. Had she been an Egyptian girl, she would never have left the shutters thrown open the way she does every day, but then again, an Egyptian girl would probably not live alone downtown. She says she needs light in order to breathe, as though she were some kind of sun-eating rose, says she wants to let the sky into the rooms, says, *I'm not naked, what is there to hide?* Said not says. She said those things once, murmured them early one Friday, and the shutters were closed because I had closed them the night before. They striped the high ceiling of the bedroom with the gray soul of dawn in infinite gradations. I had an ear between her breasts and she was petting my head, but gently, the way you'd pet a sunflower,[4] whispering, *What is there to hide?* And the doves that the doorman was breeding on the roof oohed back at her from their wooden cages, out of sight, and our legs were tangled like weeds, her heart whimpering in my ears, *What is there to hide?* How is it that the rich are surrounded by so much beauty? That hour we spent together beneath the heavened striations was kinder to me than ten years in Cairo had been—kinder, more merciful, as though I were a living creature after all, deserv-

---

4. Due to the fragility of sunflower petals, "petting sunflowers" is an expression in Beheira to denote an especially soft and cautious touch.

ing of a gentle touch. But really, it isn't me, it's her. She actually lives like this; everything from the shoes she wears to the soap in her bathroom is thoughtfully considered, has a touch of grandeur I can't explain. When we are together, some of that favor God intended for her rubs off on me by proximity. I remember that insane apartment, filled with furniture that seemed aware of itself, conscious of its signification: handwoven kilims, salt lamps, calligraphy, plants in copper cachepots that dripped their star-shaped leaves over everything. She even had a government-issued sign for Sherif Street, one of the original blue ones, rusted now with age. It had clearly been stolen and was mounted in her kitchen above the sink, and it was beautiful too. I remember how she fills her mornings with drums—Tinariwen or Alsarah and the Nubatones—how she burns incense and paints her toenails and scrubs her face with brown sugar . . . When I bring in ful[5] from a cart on the street for our breakfast, she won't eat it from the plastic bag. Arranges it on a flat clay plate, alongside apricots that she has halved, topped with ricotta, drizzled with honey, dusted in pistachios, damn-near deified before devouring. The indulgence . . . We used to sit in the wind of the balcony, celebrating the meal, me facing her, her facing this exact point on the bridge where I am standing now, certain I will see her. No one ever talks about the punishing aesthetics of being poor. The shack on the roof where I have been living for years is more outside than inside—the floor is unfinished concrete, littered with cigarette butts, broken glass, and rat pellets in the darkest corner. The mattress is without sheets, the window is without glass; I hang up a towel by feeding its corners into the holes

---

5. Ful is a popular breakfast food consisting of fava beans stewed overnight and seasoned with oil, lemon, cumin, and garlic. It is the only food in the Muslim world that it is considered unforgivably offensive to consume with the left hand, due to its resemblance in color to feces.

between the bricks, and this is how I keep out the sun. Every surface is clothed with dust. I've lived there since the death of photojournalism, since the foreigners left, taking their drugs with them, since the lines for gas and subsidized bread began. All these years, I never once complained about my little home on the roof. Only now, looking back, do I realize how terrible it is to subsist on just enough, without the joy of beautiful things.

WHERE HAVE YOU BEEN? Reem asks as casually as she can and Sami smiles. I make some noises about work and don't explain. I spent forever blowing them off when the boy from Shobrakheit was around, because it was easier to drop my new friends than to fight for them in my own home. My punishment for this coward-ice is that when he swung the table, when he left, I was alone with my relief and its complications. Even now, when I begin to think about sharing with them where I have been all these months, I am already tired, too disheartened to try. Where to begin, and will they believe me? *Can we meet in Zamalek?* I'd asked when I phoned Reem and she began to protest until Sami cut in from the back-ground, *Yeah, I want to go to Zamalek for a change. Downtown is such a whore.* He knows somehow, has intuited why I can't return to Café Riche and would rather go instead to the expensive island, where little dogs are walked by Sudanese maids and the beggars sell roses and garlands of jasmine. We eat ice cream from Koueider and then walk to Costa for coffee. We discuss how woke Solange is, compared to her sister, Beyoncé, based on their last respective albums, and I feel jumpy the whole time, looking over my shoulder like an outlaw. When Reem goes home, Sami and I remain seated over our mugs in Costa and he lights me my first cigarette. I don't smoke but I take it from him without hesitation. I've never seen him so serious before or so smug, as though he has won a bet with God. *I wanted to warn you*, he says, spreading his knees even wider so he can lean over his own heft. *That kherty[6] comes around Riche be-cause I owe him something, not because he's clean.* Sami says *he* and not the boy from Shobrakheit's name, to spare me the embarrassment.

---

6. A kherty refers to a man who provides informal services to foreigners in a range of capacities—as a broker, tour guide, travel agent, souvenir-seller, scuba diving instructor, photographer, fixer, or pimp, for example. In Cairo, they gen-erally congregate near tourist sites, such as the pyramids or downtown. The term is considered derogatory.

I almost say, *Who?* but stop myself. Lifting the cigarette to my lips, I attempt to inhale but end up dry-coughing painfully. *No, suck on it like a straw. Hold it in your mouth and then inhale,* he instructs in response. Then he begins to muse aloud that romance in Cairo is unlike romance elsewhere in the world. He lived in London till he was seven (is proud of this) and so claims he can compare. *In Cairo it's more like . . . you're bored. Every girl you meet, you think,* Hey, are you my wife? *If the answer is yes, you throw yourself at her feet. If she tries to leave, you chase her back. It's all life-and-death stuff, very dramatic, but also just a way of passing the time. Egyptian men— we're fucking loyal, and you should be worried.* He plucks the cigarette from my fingers and raises both his and mine at once, so that they poke from the sides of his lips like tusks. He takes a drag, tilts his head back, and exhales, enjoying every moment of this soap opera monologue. *It's not over, is what I'm saying.* Men love to save me. Men love to save me from other men.

HIGHS LIKE HEIGHTS. A good high demands to be experienced from a point of elevation: rooftops, balconies, bridges . . . I continue to wait for hours while the rain stops and starts and stops again. The traffic loosens its throat on the bridge. It's a losing game, this waiting on the smallest life sign from her. I stand long enough for my clothes to get soaked through and then halfway dry, long enough to remember the dialect of car horns a trucker first taught me in my father's workshop. Before the Gulf War, 18-wheelers used to drive from Aswan as far as Baghdad, and farther, sometimes stopping in Shobrakheit to get their tires patched and pressured. Two long beeps, two short beeps, one long beep is a bridal celebration. Everyone knows that. But three short, one long, one short: *You son of a fuck-er.* Two short, one short, two short, one short: *I love you, I love you,* or else *Coming through, coming through.* Does she hear talk in the car horns? Or does she think they are all just angry drivers making angry-driver sounds? Will I ever get the chance to ask her? Will she ever come out on her balcony? It's hard to know when to give up, cut my losses. The longer I wait, the greater the chance that I will see her. But the longer I wait, the longer I have been waiting on this bridge, and the higher the stakes are if I don't see her. It also seems certain, based on God's ironic bent, that she will appear the minute I turn to leave, and I cannot be made a fool like that. God is funny like that, He doesn't like me like that. I wish I had never come up here. It twists my brain to know she is somewhere in the world, breathing, making those little sighing sounds she makes when lost in thought, and I cannot know who, if anyone, is around to hear them. She is home or she is not. If she is home, she will come out or she will stay inside forever. If she is not home, she is in America already at one of those exercise classes with her mother, or at a bar in Zamalek with the English boys, drinking her wine iced like an Alexandrian sailor. Of course, she doesn't know how Alexandrian sailors add ice to their wine or how to tell sea mullet from farmed mullet;[7] how to prevent thieves and stoners from climbing onto your boat at night[8] or remove the fish-stink from your fingers after eating;[9] how to harden concrete with sugar, how to encourage a hen to lay;[10] how to speak and eat with a defensive razor blade tucked between the cheek and upper gum; how to juice a lemon without souring your hands, using the blunt edge of a knife. She knows nothing. She goes to the market and comes back with zebdiyya mangoes *in November*,[11] which she then tries to feed me. It was a fluke, her picking up the spoon from the middle that first day we sat beside each other in Café Riche. There is nothing she intuited, no generational secrets repeating themselves through her loins. She is just as much a foreigner as the ridiculous Italians and Germans I used to fuck. She is drinking her wine with ice at a bar in Zamalek out of bad luck, or else she is at home mopping the same kitchen tiles on which she once spread her legs and begged me to photograph her. What kind of an Egyptian would *do* that? Offer nudes to a man she'd known for two months? She could be all over the internet with those legs of hers. She could be on every porn site, passed around the WhatsApp groups designed for this purpose. I wouldn't even

---

7. Wild sea mullet, one of the most popular fishes in Lower Egypt, is distinguishable from its farmed counterparts by yellow "ears" and an absence of mud in the gills.

8. The surest way to prevent trespassers from boarding a boat is to anchor it midriver and braid shreds of aluminum cans into the anchor line.

9. Rubbing coconut oil on the fingers is the most popular Egyptian method, but in the smaller villages and particularly in Beheira, coconut milk is considered more effective at eliminating fish-stink.

10. Feeding a hen a mixture of dandelions and her own eggshells, crushed and toasted so as to be unrecognizable to her, will encourage the hen to lay.

11. In Egypt, zebdiyya mangoes are used exclusively for juicing and, like all mangoes, they appear in the fall and by November have largely disappeared from the markets.

need to name her—she'd be found out in days and dragged, humiliated by every level of society: strangers on the street, fruit-sellers, shopkeepers, the doorman, her colleagues and students, relatives, every single person she'd ever met. I could have made her life unbearable and she'd have no one to blame but herself . . . As usual, however, nothing bad has happened to her. With the same stroke of fortune that seems to follow her everywhere, her nudes aren't with me. My analog camera hasn't worked in years. A battery leakage ruined it in 2014 and no amount of surgery I perform will save it. She asked me to shoot her so I shot her, pretending because I wanted her to believe I could. She asked me to develop the photos so she could see them, and I promised to, over and over until she stopped asking. I'd give anything to have the evidence now, to remind myself of that night: the kitchen tiles, her goose-pimpled thighs in macro. Instead here I am standing on the 6th of October Bridge praying for a glimpse of her in the distance, clothed, in broad daylight . . . At this point, even that would be enough. I don't need to reinsert myself into her life, so long as she is safe and happy, so long as I can *know* she is safe and happy. And if she is not . . . If she is not, all I need is a glimpse.

I RETURN TO ENGLISH as if to the arms of a lover and feel instantly safe and indigenous there. *What are borders, anyway? Just lines in the sand. What are citizens? Just people fucking within the same lines in the sand—and their children and then* their *children*, I tell William, who is standing behind me in the kitchen, running his teeth along my neck while I peel and de-heart late guavas. *So let's stay within the lines*, he mumbles. *Stay?* I say. *Egypt is the squarest country in the world*, he continues, his heavy hands on my shoulders, making it more and more difficult to work a knife. *Only on a map*, I laugh, *but the women are round in all the right places.* I wiggle my hips to show which places. Then the guava juice touches my cheek because I'm melting over the counter. I return to English and find my quick wit there, right where I left it. I feel sharp again. Like a toddler in its mirror stage, aroused by recognition. That thrill of being who I am swirls around my belly. William takes the juice off my skin where it shines like spittle, laughs at my jokes because he gets them, they are *for* him. I return to English and even my breathing changes, little *oh-oh*s of ecstasy instead of *ah-ah*s. For too long I have been that other girl: weak, self-effacing—an obvious American in her fat-tongued, blubbering Arabic, and punished for it. But not anymore. It is in Arabic that lovers murder each other with side tables, and it is in English that they theorize about what it means to be murdered by side table. It is in English that they write about it, grieve and forgive, fuck their equals.

THE END IS ALSO A BEGINNING, of rummaging through memories. I see her as she was that first night. The silk dress shining and cool, wetting everything it touches with its slippery tongues. I lifted the thing off her head as fast as I could. No buttons, no zippers or lace, but seemingly many layers, each thin as a lick. The distinct impression that I was unveiling royalty from the ground up. First the feet: thin and long-toed like hands, one of them pointing inward as though whispering to the other. A little higher and the right knee stared stoically ahead, like the face of a king, while the left side-eyed it, pleadingly. When the silk was over her head, nothing but a brassiere and string-thing barely there beneath. When even these were off, I could not contain my surprise: palm-sized, watery breasts with high nipples, the aching gooseneck. Her downparts were brown and puckered the way the mouths of grapes are when plucked from their wooden clusters.[12] Swollen-heavy, fissured around the edges. I took it all in with the light of the billboards flooding in from her many balconies, with the hunger of a man returning from exile. It had been twenty years since I felt home in a woman's arms, and the effect was one of outrage. Why had it taken her so long to appear? I have always been deserving of a first-class love, A-grade, elegant, not these sloppy streetwalkers with dirt under their nails and no evidence of skeletons, just lumps and folds all over. She is almost another species, so lithe in the lines, lovely. With her I felt for the first time that I was filling my own height, rather than failing it. I was proud to walk beside her on the street and to see the Tramadol-dealers who know me by name, the shoe-sellers and mechanics from Champollion,

---

12. Using fruit, especially grapes, as sexual innuendo was popularized by the 2007 shaabi song "El ainab" by Omar Khairat, in which the speaker is a fruitseller advertising his wares in increasingly erotic and possessive language. It is usually played at Egyptian weddings, along with Khairat's equally suggestive "Az az kaboria," a song about sucking/nibbling crabmeat.

recognizing me for what I am, which is a category apart. If she knew, if she only knew how mine she is, how long I had been expecting her, she'd appear on the balcony now, put her elbows on the marble balustrade, and weep from the belly like a widow.[13] She could be weeping at this very moment, out of view; my heart hurts to imagine. I was the one who left, after all, *abandoned* her in her dreaming, without explanation or goodbye. That morning I was certain from the position of her sleeping body (her curled back walling me out, knees to chest) that she wanted me gone, but now I remember how she used to walk past my chair in the dining room, sliding my head back with four fingers so she could kiss my brow—or else only pretending to, coming at my eyes with her pecking mouth, shouting laughter, playing—and I pity the missing she must be feeling today, alone in that apartment. How many times has she passed that chair where I used to sit? Do I have an obligation to return, to fold my body on its wood and explain?

---

13. In Islamic metaphysics, the lament of a young widow is believed to be so impressive to God that he will occasionally revive her husband, granting the couple, out of pity, a few more years together. Burials are therefore delayed for as long as possible and widows encouraged to pull their hair, tear at their clothes, and rub dust into their faces.

WHY WILLIAM? SUCH A SMALL THING. When I said I had been born and raised in Michigan before moving to New York City, he raised his right palm and pointed below the thumb, saying *Detroit?* the way my father taught me to do in case I was kidnapped as a child. He should not have known to do this, because he wasn't from Michigan himself, but he knew, both the where and the how. I was so grateful to be seen that my eyes watered. When we talked, I didn't have to explain basic concepts like yoga or sushi. When I asked him, casually, as a joke, where he was when Michael Jackson died, he could answer. We were both in kitchens an ocean apart and heard it from our older siblings. What are the chances of that? He can be charming, entertaining. Not a big man, but a man with flooring BDE, an obvious alpha parting through a sea of minor men. Now he is asleep on the couch, which is as far as we made it. I leave him there drooling: British, with British teeth, all of them fighting for front row. Enormous hands that are also purple, square-nailed, lewd as meat patties. We came to my apartment because his doorman won't allow it. Now that the fun is done, though, the presence of a male in my space is nauseating. I look for reasons to resent William's body. He wears white-girl-in-India pants with elephants on them. He haggles with taxi drivers over the price of the trip before getting in the car. If the meter isn't working, he uses his fingers or types out the number he wants to pay on his phone because he hasn't bothered to learn the Arabic, despite living here for four months already. If the meter is working, he'll thumb out the exact coin instead of doing not the generous thing but the *natural* thing of rounding up to the nearest multiple of five. Two taxis swerved off, one of them swearing at us. The driver of the third agreed to take us over the 6th of October Bridge to downtown but then wrong-eyed me in the rearview mirror the whole time, trying to figure out if I was Egyptian or not—if it was him and me versus William, or him alone versus William and me. I kept quiet, looking out the window while William big-mouthed in big English about Cairo Jazz Club, where we had just spent two thousand pounds on imported liquor. The driver gently turned down the Quran fizzing from the radio, whether to eavesdrop or because he was offended, I couldn't tell. William imagines at every turn that the locals are cheating him—which they very often are, and which he deserves (*locals*, he calls them). He doesn't hear himself, slurring entitlement paranoia: a guest in this country, come temporarily, voluntarily, to shit in the coat closet, spit in every vase, accuse the furniture of imposture . . . *And what are you supposed to be?* he asks the hole in the bathroom floor.[14] Meanwhile, unlike the poorest fellah, he doesn't wash his asshole when he shits in porcelain. When we arrived at my building, I thanked the taxi driver in Arabic and doubled William's money once he'd stepped out of the car: thirty pounds. He came up to see my balconies, and that should have been the end of the night. If he hadn't thought to use his teeth in the kitchen, on my neck, I would not be stuck with his body on my couch now, this body that doesn't curl to protect its organs in sleep, but splays out like a crab, taking twice the space it needs.

14. With the exception of those at tourist sites and hotels catering to Westerners, toilets in Egypt tend to be squat toilets consisting of a toilet pan at floor level instead of a raised commode seat. Toilet paper is rarely available, since Egyptians consider it more hygienic to use a bidet.

AFTER WAITING FOR HOURS on the bridge to see her, she comes out at last. It is quicker than I expected, so fleeting that afterward I go crazy with doubt: Did I imagine it? Was I looking at the right balcony? It could have been a young boy on the sixth floor instead of the American girl on the seventh. The person appeared for about five seconds with a mobile phone at the ear, leaned over the balustrade to look at the street below, then turned and disappeared back inside. That was it. I don't know how the idea came to me to call her phone, but I find myself calling, thinking that if the line is busy, it will mean it really was her I had seen on the balcony, and if not, then not. I call as I have called a hundred times since that night she first recited her number to me in Café Riche. She recited the digits singly, saying zero, one, zero, one, eight, one, two, four, six, six, six, instead of clustering them like any Egyptian would: zero, ten, one, eighty-one, twenty-four, three sixes. For the first time since then her phone does not even ring; it appears to be switched off. I try again to be sure, but am met with the same automated message. I call twice more before my battery dies. Half an hour later, at my ahwa[15] under the bridge, I borrow Saeed's mobile to try her again and this time the line is flushed, warm-blooded. On the fourth ring, she answers: *Allo? Allo?* I choke and hand the phone back to Saeed, who says kindly, *You're lucky if your beloved is also your destiny*, a saying I've never liked and see more often on the bumpers of microbuses than anywhere else. *Thanks, Saeed.* He's wiping the plastic tables with what was definitely once a white undervest (his own). The down is hard, harder than I remember, quicker at me, as though this Palestinian budra were not cut with

---

15. In Egypt, an ahwa is a cheap outdoor café consisting of plastic or wooden chairs on the sidewalk or street, where you can order beverages and shisha. It is typically a male-dominated space.

flour after all, but pure.[16] I collapse into the plastic chair Saeed has pulled out for me, fatigued, my clothes still damp, certain, suddenly certain that her phone was never switched off. She has blocked my number as though we'd never shared a bed, as though I'd never rested my hands on her shoulders . . . She has made herself unreachable. I want to cut off these hands and throw them into the river. I want to die a blunt-edged death.

---

16. Cocaine smuggled over the border from Gaza is often cut with cheap substances like talc, chalk, milk powder, baking soda, or laundry detergent, but the most common is flour.

THERE IS A DIFFERENCE between being poor and being cheap, and William is cheap, with delusions of sophistication. *The hollandaise was just salad dressing! The bruschetta was ketchup, and they think fino*[17] *counts as a baguette.* The shrimp avocado salad he ordered came without shrimp, and the avocado itself was so far from ripe it had been peeled and chopped like a carrot. William sent it back, and the server, bowing, apologetic, having never eaten one himself, could not understand why. The avocado on William's plate was the right color, looked like the picture on the menu. How could he know it was not supposed to crunch? It's not that I've never dated a white man before—I have—but never one so oblivious to his privilege. They were usually the opposite: entrepreneurially aware, putting on street corner skits of self-flagellation and getting tipped in kisses. When I offered to pay for our meal, William suggested we split the bill, what the Egyptians call *going American*, though Americans call it *going Dutch*. This was worse than if he'd let me pay for the whole thing. The only move more disgusting—which I've seen him do in other settings—would have been to pay for exactly and only what he'd eaten. He spent the night in my apartment again but only because he ran a knuckle up my back as we stood waiting for the fourth cab to turn us down. Of course, now that his body is sprawled over my bedsheets, belly-up like something drowned, whistling through his nose hairs, I hate us both. Anytime we're together in public, I get spoken to in English and asked where I'm from. Only a foreigner in Cairo is made to repeat ten times a day: *I'm Egyptian, I'm Egyptian.* This never once happened with the boy from Shobrakheit. When we were together in public, no one would have dared ask me where I

---

17. Fino is a baguette-shaped loaf with a fine-textured, fluffy crumb and a slightly buttery-sweet taste. It is the number one staple in the Egyptian diet and is consumed at most meals.

was from, and if they had dared, he would have defended me with one of his characteristic rages. He would have cursed them up and down, calling them dogs and shoes and threatening to raise their mothers' ancestors from the ground. William, on the other hand, doesn't even realize what's at stake when I am asked by shopkeepers and street children and sugarcane-juicers where I'm from. And why should he realize? They ask him too. Those outside of a language, of a culture, see furniture through a window and believe it is a room. But those inside know there are infinite rooms just out of view, and that they can always be more deeply inside.

I HAVE A ROUTINE NOW, MIRRORING HERS. On the mornings she goes to work, I wait for her in the entrance to a building across from hers where there's a stair I can sit on and smoke. There, if I need to take my red pills,[18] the doorman will bring me a glass of water since I sometimes split one with him. She comes out wearing headphones and turns into the street without looking. From the doorway, I follow her with my eyes until she gets into a cab or an Uber. No way to be sure she is actually going to the British Council for work and not to Sami's apartment, where she will undress even before the elevator jerks to a stop at his floor so he and his little brother can take turns on her. She returns home around six or seven and I wait for her in one of two different positions. She never sees me, walks around with that tourist-oblivion, cocksure, trusting the world around her . . . On days she's not working, it's harder to monitor her comings and goings, so I don't always try. I've begun to live off glimpses. I've begun to worry at the wounds. Lipstick and the red shoe that hurts her little toe, for example, are evidence of a post-work date, later confirmed when she comes home late, so late the doorman is already asleep, the gates of the building padlocked shut, and she must take out her little shining key, fiddle with it, nervous, clearly, no one on the street but her (and me). The underside of my desire to see her is having nowhere real to go. When she is safely inside I will wander the streets for a few more hours. Ever since that first night I went up to her apartment and saw how much space there was, how high the ceilings, I have not been back to my shack on the rooftop. Once a week the bitch landlord calls and I have to lie, say I've

---

18. The "red pill" is a common euphemism for Tramadol, a prescription-only opiate analgesic that is commonly abused in Egypt and other parts of Africa due to its low price point and accessibility. Other street names for Tramadol include *chemia, strawberries, farawla,* and *rouge.*

gone to the country and will make rent when I return. I won't, of course—can't. The only thing worse than being broke in Cairo is being broke in Shobrakheit, where my mother dictates every dinner and my father never objects, where the egrets my grandmother used to feed by the river still remember me. For the last week, I've been sleeping in the mosque and spending my days sitting in various places: the ahwa under the bridge, benches along the corniche, the stationery shop on Sherif, where they let me sometimes. It helps to have a routine, but I'm dead-walking here. Beginning to smell, and I know it, my clothes growing proudly their own stains, all the stitching sighing at the lips. To dress like you have money is not just an exercise in vanity, it's also a mode of protection. This city punishes the poor every chance it gets. There is hardly a public bench left that doesn't require payment, but I once saw the American girl sit in Cilantro for two hours and leave without ordering a thing. The servers came and went, forgiving her everything because they knew she could pay if she wanted to. They could tell from her clicking shoes and leather handbag, even if she had no hair and spoke with an accent—or perhaps because of these things. I remember how she invited me once to have cheesecake at Four Fat Ladies, and when we entered the dessert place together the men stopped chewing and followed me with their jaws. They would not quit staring. *Please, join us*, I offered the entire room when the plate of cheesecake came, spreading my arms wide enough to include everyone. They hastily cleared their throats and averted their eyes, clearly ashamed to be out-gentlemanned by a tramp like me. This was all back when I took regular showers, and the American girl would wash my clothes with her own things in a machine in the bathroom and hang them out to dry on one of the balconies. I was presentable then. She scrubbed my underwear by hand to preserve the elastic. I smelled like Ariel instead of tobacco and sweat. But I try not to think of these things now.

If I entered Four Fat Ladies today, I would be met immediately by several uniformed servers, asking what I was looking for, *café or restaurant?* I don't dare try it. On the grass outside the Mogamma Al Tahrir, I lie with the other bums, warming myself on the heat of the earth, cigarette butts sprinkled around my head like pillow feathers. When I dream, I dream uneasily of tangerines, peeled and sectioned by my mother somewhere far, far away.

WHEN I FORCED MYSELF to go back to Riche for the first time in months, Sami told me Reem was worried too. *She thinks you should move in with her for a while, or at least take a break from downtown,* he said, although we both knew that Reem loved conspiracy and was not worried so much as inventing excuses to take me home. I rolled my eyes. *She thinks he might show up at your door,* he added. *Yeah, well, she also thinks Soad Hosny was pushed off a balcony, remember?* I snorted and Sami's eyebrows came together. *What?* he said blankly. *Soad Hosny,* I repeated. *Soad Hosny was pushed off a balcony,* he said and lit another cigarette while I tried to put the pieces together. *But you and Reem—the first time I met you, we were sitting right here at this table and she was saying murder and you—* He waved his cigarette in my face to shut me up. *I was only pretending to believe it was suicide so Reem could get all worked up. Even* she *knows that.* I opened my mouth to object. *You really shouldn't believe everything you hear,* he snapped, and for the first time since I'd met Sami, he seemed annoyed rather than charmed by my naïveté. I was stunned. I stood up to leave and he didn't try hard enough to stop me. Outside, the street was louder than ever. I walked home looking wildly around me, wondering what else I had gotten wrong. I watched a man open his car door while driving and couldn't tell if he had done it to spit on the ground or examine his tire. What was stopping traffic at the intersection—the officer in neon vest or the red light? Were the ficus trees dwarfs or just badly pollarded? There was a long-haired man I always saw around Hoda Shaarawy in loud parrot-colored makeup, which I'd always assumed was drag (and how heartening to see drag in Cairo!), who now suddenly looked like a woman and a prostitute. I walked through Talaat Harb Square, past souvenir shops and travel agencies, past Soliman Pasha Fruits Juice, trying to see it all with the eyes of the familiar. What I saw: flies on the fruit, a beggar on the ground with her abaya pulled back to showcase her club feet. What did the boy from Shobrakheit notice when he walked down Mahmoud Bassiouny? What did he see when he looked at me? In the apartment, I discovered the laptop I had thought was gone, pushed neatly into a corner, under the bed. I hadn't put it there, but neither had it been stolen. Why did I think it had been stolen? Nothing had ever been taken from this apartment while he was here. I left change in the copper bowl by the door and there were frequently loose hundreds in my bags and in the pockets of my clothes. Was I counting? It's difficult to say. I remember how, whenever I took out my wallet in the street, he would turn his whole body away and light a cigarette, as though I had pulled out a thong instead of the soft, fraying banknotes. As though he were ashamed of my money or performing respect for my privacy. But why do I say *performing respect* instead of *respecting*? Does the fact that I noticed his behavior around my wallet and remember it now with cinematic lucidity imply an underlying suspicion? Was I watching him from the corner of my eye for signs of theft or envy? Did he notice and is that why the money was always pointedly—aggressively, even sarcastically—where I had left it? I remember once how a twenty lay on the floor of the foyer for three days before I finally picked it up on our way out the door. But why did I leave it there? But why didn't he pick it up? The way he walked out of the room when I ordered food for us and asked the man on the phone what the total came to . . . The way he stepped over and around that twenty for three days, refusing to see it . . . Did he feel mistrusted and did I mistrust him? Was it true what he said about me? *Bourgeois*: one of the few words we didn't need to translate between us since it lay in the no-man's-land: French. Was I as classist as he wanted me to believe? Did he put the laptop under the bed in order to show it to me? Where and why have my mother's pearls gone?

TODAY MY FATHER TEXTED ME, wanting money; I laughed a good laugh, the best since the budra, and nearly smashed my phone against the sidewalk. I haven't eaten properly in days and have only two cigarettes left and one strip of the red pills that will keep me from dying of withdrawal symptoms for another week—if I ration them. I'm not a violent person, but when someone is being wronged in front of me, I can be violent. At the age of twelve, I broke a cane-farmer's wrist. I was walking home behind him and another man I didn't recognize when the farmer began to speculate on the sharpness of cunt a woman would have if widowed that young and living alone for so long.[19] I limped home an hour later with blood on my shirt and what looked like a tomato bitten out of my skull. When my grandmother learned what I had done and why, she kissed me up and down and bought me imported ice cream. I remember this as I tail the American girl from a distance. Her head is sculptural, a mannequin's, because of the shave. I see it from behind. The vertical groove at the back of her neck is deep and divisive, as if carved in stone, reminding me of the smaller groove I can't see, from her septum to that heart-shaped upper lip. All her body parts look like other body parts . . . Where is she going so early on a Friday morning? The street is empty. She's gazing up at the sky. I see it happening before it happens, because I know what to look for. I was always the one removing her purse from her outer shoulder, where it hung, tempting thieves, and pinning it instead beneath her other armpit, away from traffic. Now she walks without me and her purse dangles like an invitation. The motorcycle appears around a corner coming the wrong way down a one-way street.

---

19. In some of the smaller Egyptian provinces, legend has it that a widow who does not remarry or return to her father's house grows vaginal teeth as a form of protection against potential sexual violation.

THAT WE NEED TO BE NEEDED by the one we love is something I should have learned years ago from watching my parents. Instead it was my older sister who learned. I remember Lulu, who now lives in DC with her husband, calling me when they first slept together, in 2012, back when she was a sophomore and he was her rowing coach at George Washington. She said, *You won't believe this, but he couldn't get it in.* I laughed because I didn't imagine the relationship would ever last; Lulu was forever getting her heart broken by older, unavailable men looking for a last hurrah. *What did you do?* I asked, and she said, *I waited. He kept finding the spot, then losing his hard, then rubbing around, getting his hard, then losing the spot again. It took half an hour.* When she told me this, I was still in high school, radicalizing into an SJW of the worst variety. I was vindictive. I was egomaniacal and mean. I was accusing elderly white passengers on the train of racism or gentrification and live-streaming their reactions, to uproarious virtual applause. I was sharp as my toothbrushed edges, big as the teased-up afro I eventually shaved so as to pass at the gay bars I had begun to frequent as something of a Twitter celebrity. This is the question I get once a week in Cairo, now that it's clearer to people I'm not ill: *Why did you shave your head?* The answer as Manhattan as I am: identity capitalism. Because I wanted to win by appearing to have lost, because queerness is a *spectrum*, and no one can say I'm not. I wanted in. I had given up bras and armpit-shaving much earlier—to my mother's horror—and remember making a bad joke on the phone with Lulu about her coach's fragile masculinity. Lulu replied with the verbal equivalent of a shrug. *I let him do the man-thing. Sometimes I pretend to be nervous going home at night, so he will walk me to my door. He likes it and I like him liking it.* She was always smarter and kinder than me, in a way that the age difference did not account for. I remember vividly her magnanimity with men, how she protected their balloon-pride from puncture, and I can't help but wonder: Did I emasculate the boy from Shobrakheit with my independence? The irony is that I *do* need him. Only in his absence do I realize how much his arm pretzeled through mine protected me on the streets of downtown Cairo, his looming, shaggy-headed shadow signaling to other men in the vicinity that I was spoken for, that I *had a people at my back*, as he used to say, and could not be harassed without serious consequence. Now, alone at night, and especially on Mahmoud Bassiouny Street, I fall prey to hordes of Famous[20] boys roaming around with mushroom coifs, Nordic sweaters over noodly jeans. They make animal sounds at me and call my head another head good for sucking. Or else they do the less obvious, equally violating thing, which is to turn around as I approach them, so they can check my ass out when I pass by. Was it always this bad? I can't remember. This is how I ended up with William on my couch the first time. I asked him to walk me home and he wanted, instead, to ride.

20. *Famous* refers to an Egyptian trend that gained popularity in 2014 and 2015, whereby young men (often teenagers) are photographed in urban spaces wearing form-fitting fashion, elaborate hairstyles, and light makeup such as eyeliner and lipstick. These photographs are circulated on Facebook groups in the hopes that they will propel the men to internet fame or even modeling contracts. The actor, rapper, director, and screenwriter Ahmed Mekky began his career in this way.

SNATCHES IT, of course, by its long, loose strap, as you might snatch a hen from the coop by its neck. She is so stunned she doesn't even shout, just freezes with her arm outstretched as though to call the purse back, and my body is tripping toward her before I know it. The motorcycle whips around the next corner, the purse swinging from the rider's fist. She is beginning to recover from the shock, just beginning to turn her head, take a step or two when I spill backward, into the alley, out of view. The same instinct that had pushed me out into the light hauled me back by the scruff of the neck, and with the same exigent wisdom. Like climbing a ladder, hand over hand, premise to premise, until—fact: the purse is gone. What can I do for her now? This is not my entrance. If I am going to reappear, give away my position after so many weeks of shadowing her, I'll come as a savior, fortuitous, deserving of a thousand thankful kisses, not as a commiserating bystander: *Boohoo, your purse was stolen, let me stretch an arm down the street with you— Also, I just* happened *to be here on your corner at this hour?* Hell no. That's not my comeback. I need something different . . . This is how my fantasies of real injury began. Some kind of street assault, obviously, because the setting would need to be accessible to me, and what other injury requires a savior? An assault, then. Petty or sexual? Definitely sexual.

MY HANDBAG WAS STOLEN TODAY, and the funniest part is that the fool will probably take the wallet and trash the bag, not knowing the bag is worth a hundred times as much—*almost exactly* a hundred times as much. Original Fendi, limited edition: a gift from Mother, obviously, who is always trying to glam me up because she doesn't understand the aesthetic of turtlenecks under slip dresses, septum piercings, chokers—which she calls *dog collars*—silk turbans, baby hairs raked to the forehead in the shape of ocean waves . . . She was always the one to say out loud what everyone on our street was thinking, what even my own friends at Columbia hesitated to say to my face. When I braided my hair: *But this makes you look Black.* When I shaved the braids off: *But you look like a lesbian.* My poor mother meant it to be a warning, as in, *Careful, you're underselling yourself.* She couldn't imagine that I was doing so on purpose. For clout. At the time I don't think I could have explained it either, the clash of cancel culture with a sudden diversity fetish, slacktivism as the new aesthetic, the student drama at Columbia . . . How do you explain desirability politics to your whitewashed immigrant mother as she suffers through a midlife divorce? I didn't even try. Now, after all these months apart, I think I've found an approximate metaphor that would speak to her. *It's a fashion accessory, Mama. Oppression as handbag.* What is more accurate: *Oppression as shield and battering ram*, but the military metaphor won't work with her . . . In my freshman year at Columbia, I saw an elderly Finn in a wheelchair leave a panel on disability, in tears, because he was called out for taking up more time than the other speakers—both women, one Desi and one Caribbean. I've seen a Somali refugee (male, straight-identifying) booed off a spoken-word stage for mentioning rape without a trigger warning. Two Saudi sisters on the board of Columbia's MSA were caught on Snapchat saying that only native Arabic speakers can access the full nuance of the Quran; though they were both formally denounced for their Arab-supremacist comments, neither the ISAC nor the BSA nor even SJP will collaborate with the MSA to this day. This kind of public execution usually happens to newcomers who have not yet learned the rules of the discourse, but not always. My ex Elijah lost two thousand followers overnight when someone found a photo of him in the eighth grade wearing an Indian headdress for Halloween. He got dragged for weeks. In my last semester it happened to me, too, before I deleted my social media accounts and went off the grid for good. A minor celebrity accused me of Blackfishing in a Tweet that got 17.7K likes within the first eight hours. It was the lowest point in my life. Going offline wasn't even enough; people recognized me on campus. Remembering that day now from across a great body of water, it seems as silly from here as it was truly frightening and legitimate over there. In Cairo, all I want is to blend in. I spend the rest of the day canceling credit cards over the phone, wondering if I have been robbed because I look like a foreigner, or robbed because I don't look enough like one. I spend all night dreaming that Kendrick Lamar has stolen my hair and run away rapping over his shoulder, *Bitch, be humble, lil' bitch, sit down.*

SHE'LL BE WEARING THE PLEATED SKIRT that is opaque only for the first few inches and then sheer the whole way down. She won't walk on legs; she'll float on leg-shaped silhouettes, and the nude shower curtain suggestion of her lower half will encourage imaginings of her upper half—breast slope, horizons of shoulder on either side of her neck. She'll drift home from Bab El-Louk past midnight like I taught her to do, carrying black bags of sugar apples, *black*, not clear, like I taught her to do.[21] She'll be cutting through that silly one-man alley at Le Grillon, tight enough that two people coming from opposite directions must turn and brush chests to let each other pass, tight enough to frame her like a closet mirror. This is the alley where the shoe-sellers are, but of course, they will not be there. The one who gets her will be a balding mechanic from Champollion, a tire-runner, chloroform-sniffer, who couldn't light a cigarette in the wind if he tried.[22] He'll cup a hand across her face, smearing her lipstick—she'll hum her scream, inhale the grease of his finger-webbing, go limp in his grip as though shot in the ankles. I'll kill him. Beat him unconscious, head against the steel edge of an electrical box, then I'll help her put her clothes back on and carry her crying the whole way home.

---

21. In Shobrakheit, as in all the smaller provinces, it is common to sell vegetables in opaque bags so as not to incur *hasad*, or the evil eye. In the Islamic tradition, hasad is a curse that Muslims perform on each other by staring at their victim. It is often inspired by envy, hence the practice of hiding purchases from strangers.

22. Popular among Egyptians is the joke that anyone who can't light a cigarette in the wind also can't fuck in the dark. It is considered an indicator of overarching incompetence.

AT THE AGE OF SEVEN, I came home crying, *Are we Black or white?* The kids at school wanted to know. *What an idiotic question. Omar, come listen to your daughter.* In the absence of any real parental guidance, I became Latina and floated on the periphery of the Puerto Rican girl clique from which I inherited Spanish and an obsession with fingernail piercings and anti-frizz. Only once we moved from Michigan to New York, once I developed breasts and met Elijah, did I graduate into a Lite-Brite, and milk it with a vengeance for all the rejection I'd experienced in my childhood. My best friend Elijah, former boyfriend Elijah, a bearded, depressive Black man from Philly, Skip Gates's godson—yes, *that* Elijah from Twitter, the one responsible for the viral #igot99problemsandtheyareallwhite from 2014 . . . He came from a family of academics and activists who made sure he was radicalized before his milk teeth had fallen out. He'd watched every season of *Roots* by the time he was five. His older sister cowrote an article with Opal Tometi, and he'd been inside her house. We met at a listening party for The Internet in some Brooklyn warehouse. I was sixteen. It had rained and my hair was ruined, three times its usual size, electrified. He wore a leather thong around his neck with a pendant of Africa outlined in silver. When I said *Egypt*, he called me a *Black queen*, and I didn't correct him. It was the first thing he said and afterward there was no way to backtrack or explain that, actually, I was Arab. On the US census form, I check the box "other." (Both my parents check the box "white.") I didn't correct him, because on some level, I wanted to be let in. I sensed that he needed to believe I was light-skinned to feel right dating me. For all his talk of Black love between Black bodies, he liked me. He liked girls that *looked* like me: Desis, Arabs, Blasians, and other mixed chicks who were pigmented enough to be lassoed into a broad category of Blackness, if he chose to, if he named them queens before they could name themselves, dark enough not to feel like an outright betrayal of his people or his politics or his self. I have the kind of skin lazy white writers refer to with food items: honey, latte, almond, cinnamon, caramel, et cetera. We dated for two years before realizing we looked better than we ever felt together. The entire time, I wore my hair in crochet braids piled on my head like a basket, or a diadem.

IN ONE VERSION, she is on a felucca, the only female on the water for a hundred meters in any direction. There are four of them taking turns on her when I heave my body over the side of the boat and lump-roll like a log across the faux kilim floor. I slit them one by one with the razor hidden between my cheek and gums. The synthetic fabric of the kilim drinks nothing at all: it is practically plastic, made in an hour by machines the size of houses. The blood puddles and pools at the bottom of the felucca. In the river, a red cloud blooms in every direction, the birds circling overhead scream murder, and the moon blinks twice before closing her eye. When it's over, I wrap the American in my oversize coat, which is clean and damp from the swim, and pet her hair, kiss her dollhead. It takes years for her to feel safe afterward, but we do it together. I hold her to sleep every night of our lives and we heal each other . . . In another version, she is caught in a post-football-match riot, Ultras Ahlawy[23] pressing up against her, reaching for a shred of her clothes, a tit-pinch, meat-grab from the nice, thick part of her thigh. Her screams are inaudible over the roar of foghorns. The smell of sex blares across the sky. I war my way through to her, digging past two hundred men to the center of the crush, and shield her body with mine. They trample me to death, but when the police come at last, they extract her, safe, naked as a tangerine, from inside my pored, pitted skin. In another version, she answers the apartment door in her silly little slip of pajamas and the Faiyumi doorman cannot control himself. I kill him too. Repeated blows. Metal coatrack to the crown of his head, scarves and hats flying. There are so many versions of this story, I am ready for them all.

---

23. Ultras Ahlawy is a group for extremist fans of the Premier League football club Al Ahly. It is known for its pyro displays, political muscle, murderous rioting, and synchronized dance rituals, the latter considered to be the secret to its unbridled success.

So maybe I can forgive the boy from Shobrakheit for trying to crack my skull open with the steel leg of the red side table, but can I forgive him for all the hours he sat watching YouTube videos, smoking while I peeled onions in the kitchen? An American girl peeling onions for a boy from Shobrakheit? I cannot. Why, then, is my conscience chewing in my ears? I have time, in his absence, to worry the wound, and I do. Why did he choose me in the first place? And I do *feel* chosen. He chased after me. If he wanted an American girl, he could have found a proper freckled blonde with bouncing ponytail; there are enough of them tramping around downtown with their calves and armpits bare, doing "research," learning Arabic, romanticizing even the garbage heaps, the fleas on every weasel. And if he wanted an Egyptian, why not a home-grown goose who can hang on to his elbow when they walk the corniche, hide her mouth when she smiles, and practically die of giddiness when he steals an elevator kiss? Was it because I was neither of him nor truly other? Not family and not quite stranger—a thresholded, half-inside, half-outside woman? I've dated enough to understand how I am used by men who reject themselves: it's a hyphen-trick. With Elijah, it was the same. The boy from Shobrakheit wanted an in-betweener. A foreigner would be too obvious a symbol of Empire, come in crop top to colonize his body; she'd be out of his league, historically humiliating. To sleep with her would be treasonous at best. On the other hand, a real Egyptian doesn't work either. Self-loathing bleeds out beyond his self until the idea of taking a compatriot lover feels paradoxically beneath him, a waste of his potential—he'd be selling short. With me, he gets the cream of both worlds. I *am* Egyptian—recognizable but also improved by Western inflection, carrying in my fashion sense and orthodontically straight teeth the whiff of opportunity, opulence, and pride. From kissing-distance, his reflection in my eyes is one of triumph, a boy worthy of first world love. His entire generation is scrambling to get out; anyone who can leave the country has left already for Europe. Men his age are no longer granted tourist visas anywhere, because they cannot be counted on to return. Too many of them burn their passports upon arrival, too many have begged asylum at the feet of Germans and Swedes, claiming they are persecuted by the Egyptian government for homosexuality or journalism. Those that are granted asylum start YouTube channels and Snapchat accounts where they walk down the streets of their new homes gloating in Arabic, pointing out ordinary things like bicycle lanes, PDA, dogs in purses, pigeons in parks that people feed instead of eating, four different kinds of recycling bins, six kinds of milk substitute . . . Those denied asylum often find other ways not to return. They slip like rats into the underground and are never seen again. The boy from Shobrakheit used to swear to anyone who'd listen that even if he had a million pounds, he'd never leave this country. He denounced everyone who did leave as traitorous sons of whores and shoes. But sometimes, late at night, in bed with the lights off, he used to ask me quietly what it was like "outside." That's how he talked about the rest of the world— "outside," as though this country were a broom closet, as though I were a fish-eye peephole. I knew that when I wasn't home he spent hours every day watching YouTube videos of parkour, bull-fighting, skydiving, flash mobs, self-driving cars, amateur salsa, Olympic racewalking, industrial machines shelling pumpkin seeds, train-mooning, yarn-bombing, Japanese game shows, surfing, rain-forest documentaries . . . And whenever we were intimate, he closed his eyes and I couldn't shake the feeling that he was using my body for the same escapist purpose: ramming in—in hopes of getting out.

LAST NIGHT I WENT TO FIND SAMI to get back the equipment he had borrowed, pretending I didn't know that he'd lost it years ago to some nipple with cinematic aspirations. In turn, he pretended he didn't know I knew. Since 2013, this is the ruse we've been passing back and forth between us like a joint,[24] since I have no way of pressuring Sami and he has no incentive to pay me back the cost of the equipment. Only now is the loss really hurting me, and we can both see it. I need the money. The equipment was worth seven thousand pounds then, and now would sell for an easy twenty thousand, since the floating of the pound. When he saw me at the entrance of Café Riche there was a moment of nonrecognition. He turned on me with his rimless spectacles lower than usual on his nose and seemed about to say something rude and rejecting when the math finally worked out and he subtracted dishevelment from a face he used to know. I realized only then how bad I must look. He lied and told me he'd have the equipment for me next week, and I lied and said I'd come by for it on Saturday. He tried to give me some money then—two hundred pounds—but I raised my voice and threatened to turn over the table. He brought me food from the kitchen instead. A leg of lamb with raisins and cinnamon-rice, which I ate from slowly only after he begged and swore for me to do so. This was last night, and today a woman crossed the street in broad daylight to avoid passing me on the sidewalk,[25] so it's official. I've entered a new social category. I've been downgraded from a Dahab hippie—one of those *revolution-kids*, as they call anyone with big hair, a creative type, bohemian, probably vegetarian, eccentric but ultimately harmless—to . . . a hobo. Someone who looks like

---

24. This is a reference to the common Arabic saying "A shared joint lasts twice as long."

25. There is a highly contagious strain of mange called *garab* that flares up each spring among the homeless population in Cairo, causing people to take extreme measures to avoid contact with them.

he sleeps on the street, and in fact does. For years, the saving detail about me was the camera, which I wore around my neck anytime I went out. It gave my sloppiness a flair that made people hesitate to treat me like dirt. I could be very poor or possibly very rich and just eccentric—there was no way to know. People used to speak to me so carefully and now they disappear me instead. I left the camera, along with a plastic bag of clothes, at the ahwa under the bridge with Saeed because I was afraid someone at the mosque would steal it while I was sleeping. Not that it works, anyway. Saeed's the only one who has not begun to treat me with the resentment that people reserve for beggars, or the fear that they reserve for long-haired men who have not bathed in weeks. He brings me a coffee anytime I come by and sits with me if business is slow, offers me a cigarette. It is a thousand times kinder than Sami's leg of lamb, so kind I want to cry. He even offered me a job, but I can't—how can I? At the ahwa where they know my name, where anyone can see me . . . I wouldn't be my grandmother's grandson if I took a job like that. She had a richness in herself that she bequeathed to me. I was the only one who didn't flinch at her suicide by oven.[26] I was the only one who had in fact been waiting for it. How can a woman who has lived with such dignity all her life be reduced to rations from her own daughter's hand? How can the grandson of such a woman take a job serving coffee? It's bad enough that I've entered this new category. She'd die all over again if she knew. As soon as that woman crossed the street to avoid me the other day, I realized something else as well: in the story where the American girl is saved from an assault, she is saved from someone who looks like me.

---

26. In the country, even the humblest houses are equipped with ovens large enough to roast a goat whole. Unlike in Cairo and Alexandria, where throwing oneself off a balcony is the classic suicide method, in the country, houses are at most three stories high, so the more common practice is suicide by oven.

THE MOST DEPRESSING KIND OF RELATIONSHIP is one without clearly demarcated roles of victim and abuser, where the partners take turns leading, as in a Madrid-style schottische. They trade weapons back and forth beneath the table. I watched my parents do it for years. For as long as I can remember, my mother power walked over my father, reminding everyone that the apartment was in her name, that she had given him the money to jump-start his own clinic, that my father could barely afford shoelaces when she met him, and that he thought an oyster fork was just kid-sized, et cetera. Meanwhile, he successfully managed to convince her she had as much sex appeal and capacity for enlightenment as a coatrack. In order to maintain this accusation, he began what he called *a journey of knowledge-seeking* involving meditation retreats on the weekends and night courses on everything occult: alchemy, astrology, homeopathy, even tarot reading . . . She called him a fraud, he called her fat and uninspired. He refused to need my mother the way she longed to be needed, would not give the gift of jealousy or even touch her as he retreated into the world of energies and stars. She doubled her spinning at Equinox, began using chemical peels on her face, and took up ax-throwing to relieve stress. She invited a carousel of men into our home, colleagues two decades younger than her, with all their hair. My balding father greeted them formally and left the apartment, not because he trusted her but because his greatest weapon was this act of indifference. That was how my sister and I knew it was the beginning of the end for them. We spent years waiting for the divorce, even trying to egg them on with it. Instead, my mother threatened my father more explicitly with cuckolding; he would unlock the front door to find a stranger with his hand deep-diving down her blouse. She sent herself anonymous bouquets of roses. She left one of her lacy shelf bras under his side of the bed. I never told the boy from Shobrakheit about this. He had old-fashioned ideas about monogamy and love, seemed to pride his grandmother on her eternal widowhood. I knew instinctually that he would tuck away the truth about my parents' marriage and sharpen it behind my back. But I told William, who then laughed at my mother with me. This felt good at the time—we were drunk—but the next day I felt I had betrayed her. At some point even the rivalry between my parents stopped. Rather than pretending not to care, my father genuinely stopped caring, and this was the end of the end. He would open the front door and walk right past my mother and her latest accomplice. By this point, he was so consumed by planets, the nightly expressions of dreams upon his patients' teeth (i.e., grinding), the alignment of their jaws, their breathing pathways, chakras, rising signs . . . Question: How much vanity does it take to be a healer? Answer: an astrological amount.

SHE WAS THROWING GRAPES AT ME in an unfamiliar kitchen. I was catching and eating them with both hands. And then she started throwing knives. She threw them handle-first for me to catch. And then she started throwing knives that would boomerang around the room and come back to her, still handle-first. The knives would circle the room like robins, catching the light, ringing me in. She wanted to show me how to do the trick, but I'm not a good enough catch, and I told her so. *I'll hurt myself. I'm not a good enough catch.*[27] I wake up and go to sleep again. I'm so tired I can sleep anywhere: standing in a corner with my head against the wall, hunched over my knees on a metro seat, flat on the mosque floor with the carpet's fug in my lungs. My pants would be at my ankles if I didn't hold them up from inside the pockets. I have to walk wide at the knees as though wading through sewage. It's been weeks since I made it up the bridge to see my love on her balcony. I'm scared the incline will faint me if I try, and I no longer trust a population that doesn't look me in the eye to remove my body from the fly-humming sun. Every day I think about the camera still with Saeed at the ahwa under the bridge, the dearest thing I own. I could sell it and rent a digital one that actually works. I could make some money doing family portraits in Orman Garden, or go to Abdeen and take nudes of the girls with pornographic ambitions, Salwa or her sister with the sweet cauliflower ear. I could visit Sami's uncle at the newspaper and see if they need a photographer. He used to call once a month, back in 2013, begging me to cover this or that parliamentary meeting. I could wait

---

27. According to the Islamic science of dream interpretation, a knife represents a servant in the house who strives to benefit his master. Its sharpness represents the effectiveness of his master's commands, or his master's magnanimity and distinct personality. If a woman sees herself carrying a knife or gives someone a knife in a dream, it represents her love for a famous person. A pencil-sharpening knife in a dream represents a writer.

plastic tables with Saeed or at another ahwa a hundred kilometers from here where no one knows my name . . . The American girl told me her first job in New York was serving coffee, but I don't believe her. Even if it's true, she's hiding something about it, I don't have the whole picture—and even if it's true, I don't think I can do it. I can't do any of these things. My grandmother spoiled me by giving me a pride beyond my means. She raised me to believe that wherever I went I would be recognized, I would be rewarded, celebrated, and only now do I see. It was an accident, but she handicapped me to a lifetime of scoffing at the very things I need. There is such a thing as princely poverty.

TRULY THE MOST DEPRESSING KIND OF RELATIONSHIP is one where the blood runs in both directions and it's unclear who is to blame. While necking, I sink my teeth into his shoulder and pass back the venom I received from him. If the boy from Shobrakheit was controlling, it's because he felt more emotionally invested than I did, and therefore more precarious. If he felt precarious, it's because he was. Even though I wasn't counting the pounds in my wallet every morning for signs of theft, I made clear to him in other ways that our arrangement was transient, that he was *an experience*, like tonguing a thigh-gapped ballerina on spring break or doing acid in the hairy woods of Ontario. In fact, I did not even resent his mooching, because I understood that everything has a price. It is an experience to date a man who used to suck on his grandmother's teats in a village no one has ever heard of. To share secrets in a new language, to walk through the grunge of downtown Cairo learning where the cheapest liver sandwich carts are, which mosques will let you sleep in them if you have nowhere else to go, how to hand-wash socks, how to grill tuna by emptying a can with all its oil onto a napkin and setting the whole thing on fire, army-style. It's true that he ghosted me, but only after having reached the end of his utility. He saved himself the unnecessary degradation of being rejected, and he saved me from having to watch. Still, I was surprised because he's otherwise so romantically naive. Maybe all Egyptians are. Reem is the same. They think dating is about love, when any New Yorker will tell you that dating is a martial art. It's basic offense and defense. As with any contact sport, the proximity may coincidentally transform strangers into intimates, but this is not its primary intention. In English there's an entire vocabulary for the purpose of analyzing minute tactics and maneuvers: *negging, benching, breadcrumbing, gaslighting, orbiting, ghosting, haunting,* et cetera. The subcategories are extensive. William, for example, walked into my body with the same tools I possess. We are in agreement about what is happening and what is not. We'll mess around with each other until one of us finds a better offer. Then we'll split. Easy. I introduced him to Sami and Reem at Reem's house party. Naturally, they were impressed, his British accent being what Sami's aspires to be, and his shitty French giving Reem plenty of opportunity to tease and correct him. They put on a good show. *So white meat's the flavor now?* Reem yelled drunkenly in Arabic. She was rolling a joint on the back of a book while I watched. Having discovered that Sami had lit my first cigarette, she was eager to claim another first for herself. *You've had your fill of dark meat already? I'm no drumstick, but if you wanted an* ethnic *experience, I'm Egyptian, too, born and bred. My grandfather is even from Aswan—tell her, Sami*, she yelled, but she was in a good mood and so was Sami. He and William were nearby talking about Max Holloway. Reem lit the joint and then, while I watched, stuck the lit end in her mouth, closing her lips around the middle and hollowing her jaw. She motioned for me to come closer. I backed away, terrified of the ash that might already be spicing over her raw tongue. The joint was the length of my smallest finger. She motioned with more urgent hand-flapping and her mouth was clearly smiling despite the smoking tip inside it. William and Sami and all the other guys nearby noticed us and began to shout. I leaned in at last, kissed the filter-tip of the joint, and Reem blew smoke into my lungs.[28] It was exactly as pornographic as you'd expect. Everyone began to drum against the walls and tabletops, laughing and whooping. I coughed for two minutes nonstop. Not long afterward, this Jordanian who'd been

---

28. In Egyptian slang, the very last puff on a joint is commonly called *akher bossa*, the last kiss. It's a tradition particularly in the underground music scene, where joints are passed around large groups, for the last puff to be shared between either two women or a man and a woman in this way. Akher bossa is never shared between two men, for obvious homophobic reasons.

watching us walked over and whispered something in Reem's ear. She laughed and her gaze went down the Jordanian's body, to her feet and all the way back up. Sami put on the Cola song everyone loved and cranked the volume as high as the speaker system would allow. William led me by the arm to a bathroom at the end of the hall. Everyone had a good time. We woke up the next day at noon, scattered all over the apartment, in surprising positions and couplings.

I HARDLY LEAVE THE MOSQUE AT ALL ANYMORE. I sleep in a corner and sometimes wake up to find that someone has left me a bag of ful or a little money, even once a hibiscus flower.

IT HAPPENED QUICKLY. I had both hands in my jacket pocket and was walking home alone when an arm noodled through mine the way a father's might, very casually. And then, before I could register that a stranger on the street was touching me, there was someone else bullying past me from behind, his shoulder skimming mine, the rush of air making my tassel earrings swing. There he was: the boy from Shobrakheit, as if back from the grave. I recognized him by his height and hair, although now he was also wearing an oversize army coat, and rolling around on the ground with the balding man, who came out of nowhere and noodled his arm through mine. I understood all this intuitively, as though I had been waiting for it to happen: a stranger's attack, an old, familiar defender. The two of them are on the ground now and the boy from Shobrakheit slugging the man repeatedly in the side of his skull, shouting words I don't know. They are both filthy, panting, rolling around in the dirt. And then, because people in Cairo love to play peacemakers almost as much as they love to play heroes, a few Famous kids from nearby come running and one of them pulls the boy from Shobrakheit up to a standing position and the other two shield the bald man, who rolls back and forth on the ground before rocking up onto all fours and barking like a dog in my direction—barking and snarling at *me* and not at his attacker. I freeze. Despite having lived in New York City for fifteen years, this is the most terrorized I have ever been on a street. The man shakes his hairless plastic head and barks in the wrong direction.

WHEN IT FINALLY HAPPENS, all I can think is, *This is it, this is it.* It's the first time I've left the mosque in a week. She's late returning home, walking with such purpose that her clothes flag out straight behind her. She parts the black air with her long red skirt, hands in pockets, elbows angled out like wings. The street is empty, so late at night it is early morning, only a young couple walking with their arms interlaced ahead of her, a few Famous kids preening for photos, and an ugly man, bald as a urinal,[29] circling a drain nearby. Then suddenly he stops circling and begins to beeline toward her back, catching up to my own expectation and *this is it*! I am a few steps behind when his hand reaches for her waist in a curling motion, and this is my cue. I step into the streetlight. Then I don't know what happened. *What happened? Tell me what happened.* One of the Famous kids is leading me away, his arm around my shoulder. A concerned stranger, asking me in a kind, soft voice what happened. But I don't know what happened. My heart is leaping out of my chest. The American girl is also there, stunned, her mascara bruising both her eyes, and someone is shouting, making it difficult to hear anything: *He grabbed her, he grabbed her arm!* And then I realize it is my voice shouting, drowning everyone out, *We were walking and he grabbed her!* The Famous kid turns to the girl, respectfully, with his eyes lowered. *Miss, is this true?* She nods once and he looks at me meaningfully. *Listen, we'll take care of that bum, he's drunk, look at him—he thinks he's a dog. We'll deal with him, but you have a woman with you and it's late. Take her home, my friend.* I don't even know how I heard these words, I was still shouting but more feebly now, shaking uncontrollably, *He grabbed her . . .* He grabbed her but

---

29. In the Egyptian dialect, the word *bald* is slang for *urinal*, making it offensive. The polite way to describe a bald man is to refer to him as *shorn*, implying that his hairlessness is a choice of personal grooming.

now the Famous kid is rubbing the back of my skull like a brother, the first physical contact I've had in months, saying, *You did the right thing, you did the right thing, and we'll finish the bum off, but you have a woman with you, take her home.* He's leading me away by the shoulder.

IT WAS CLEAR TO ANYONE WATCHING that the barking man was unwell. When the boy from Shobrakheit first tackled him, he didn't seem to notice, and then on the ground his responses were delayed and inappropriate. I once knew a Libyan deli owner who spoke fluent Spanish when drunk and not a word of it when sober, but to confuse one's own species is evidence of more than intoxication. Hours later, replaying the incident in my mind, I remembered that when I first turned onto Mahmoud Bassiouny Street, there had been a couple strolling ahead of me, the man with his hood up and the woman in a dark hijab, so that from behind they looked like matching tortures: a romance. They had been walking arm in arm when the bald man saw me, a bald woman in a red dress, and came to be my walking partner. We looked the part. I had closely shaved my head that very day and it gleamed in the streetlight. He had not been trying to harm me, that much was obvious. But after being tackled to the ground and bloodied by someone else, he continued to bark at my back as I walked in the direction I lived with the boy from Shobrakheit. It's hard to explain what was happening between us once the shock was over. We weren't speaking to each other, just walking side by side, walking home as we had walked home a hundred times, and there was no Arabic in me at all anymore and he didn't know that yet, but I knew. My English body led the way, silent and controlled, analyzing from my position as damsel-in-distress this display of machismo on my behalf. He had beat a sick man sicker and would now be expecting a reward. He was still panting, sweating as though he'd run ten miles, and maybe he had, to get where I was. His clothes were torn and filthy from rolling on the ground, and beneath the blood and the sweat there was a tremble that he tried to hide by opening and closing each of his fists. He was triumphant, the tremble euphoric. We got to the entrance of my building and he stopped as though to take leave. *I'll make us some tea*, I said, and it was all the permission he needed to speak. *Are you okay?* he asked. *I'm okay*, I said, fumbling with the key to the building lock. *That man came—he just came out of nowhere and attacked you from behind. If I hadn't—but you—how are you feeling?* I swung open the building's gate. *I just don't want you to be frightened*, he continued, and it was clear to any American girl that he wanted me to be frightened. *I just don't want you to be upset. I'd never let anyone upset you. I'd never let a woman that I—any woman that I know be humiliated like that*, he said, and he was watching me earnestly in the elevator mirror, hoping I would be humiliated like that. He was a shade darker than I had remembered him being and his cheekbones glinted beneath the light like two scissored boning knives. I pulled apart the accordion door of the elevator and stepped out of confinement, feeling him follow. *I don't feel humiliated, he was drunk and also clearly—* I began to say, unlocking the front door of my apartment, but he cut me off. *So anyone who's drunk can grab you and you're fine with it?* I kicked off my shoes and left him at the entrance to shut the door behind him, and my English brain knew that in Arabic he'd be offended at having to follow me into my own home and close the door behind himself while I walked off. If we had still been together he would never have allowed it. He would have shouted for me to come back and answer him. Or he would have left the door open so I'd have to close it myself, but his new position was fragile and uncertain. My English brain didn't want to cede any ground just yet. There are calculations that precede thought, there are protective measures that one recognizes as protective only retrospectively. I defended myself with an instinct that was not there before. *The man barked. He wasn't only drunk, he was unwell*, I announced in the kitchen as I flicked on the kettle and brought down mugs from the cupboard. How to say *mental health* in Arabic? *Sick, he looked sick, and anyway he didn't hurt me.* I brought out two tea bags and their strings wound around each other, they wouldn't let go. He could not contain himself: *I've never met anyone as cold as you, you're not human, you're not even a woman. A stranger attacked you and you're not even upset, I'm still shaking and you*— I spooned out the sugar, then opened the fridge door for a sprig of fresh mint.

THIS IS A DRINKING GAME. The first person asks the second: *Wanna buy a dog?* The second person asks the first: *It barks?* The first person tells the second: *It barks.* The second person asks the third: *Wanna buy a dog?* The third person asks the second: *It barks?* The second person asks the first: *It barks?* The first person tells the second: *It barks.* The second person tells the third: *It barks.* The third person asks the fourth: *Wanna buy a dog?* The fourth person asks the third: *It barks?* The third person asks the second: *It barks?* The second person asks the first: *It barks?* The first person tells the second: *It barks.* The second person tells the third: *It barks.* The third person tells the fourth: *It barks.* If there is no fifth person for the fourth person to ask, he asks the first: *Wanna buy a dog?* This is an Egyptian drinking game, not an American drinking game with cards and Ping-Pong balls. In America, no one wants to buy a dog, all the dogs are rescued. The buses and trains drive themselves and when an ambulance comes through everyone moves out of the way. You can be a woman or a man or neither in America. All the parks are free and they restrict the nicotine content in their cigarettes to protect their citizens from addiction. You can be stabbed to death on a street surrounded by people and no one will help you. You can be molested by a stranger in public and then get up, go home, and make tea, remembering how many sugars everyone takes and to save the tea bags as food for the houseplants, putting them on an upturned jar lid by the sink, because one use is not enough in America. They must also be disemboweled and buried in dirt.[30]

---

30. Slums in Cairo are often dependent for survival on the waste of wealthier adjacent neighborhoods, who consider it good ethic to throw away clean bags of food. Even tea bags are dug out of the trash and reused, just as cigarette stubs are collected and sucked down to the filter. It is considered selfish for those with useful trash to repurpose it themselves.

AND THEN, just as I came to pour the hot water, he spoke in a voice that was smaller than I'd heard it in my mind all these months, his child voice, the voice he used in bed when all the lights were out and he wanted to ask me something threatening to himself. He said, *Did you ever love me?* I wasn't prepared for this and the water scalded me, I missed the mugs entirely. Behind my back, I felt the kitchen empty of him, and I remembered suddenly and for no clear reason that he loved Fernando Pessoa, the films of Volker Schlöndorff, Wim Wenders, and Jacques Rivette, the ballooning, childish portraits of Jean Dubuffet's early works, particularly *Woman Grinding Coffee*, which he had printed on a little card in his wallet. I remembered how he could date any photo you showed him that had been developed within the country based on the quality of paper and ink. I remembered how he knew all the street kids on Champollion by name and how they came to him for candy and sometimes gave him things: stickers, broken toys, a miniature bottle of glitter nail polish, which he happily painted on his thumbnail. *What have I done? What have I turned him into and what else have I forgotten?* I went out to find him and he was sitting sideways on the wooden chair of the dining table, hunched over. He jumped up when he saw me, and when I approached with my arms outstretched, he quickly stepped back with a panic I didn't recognize. *It's me,* I said, taking another step forward. *Please,* he said, looking down at his coat, *I don't want to get you dirty.* Something was wrong. *I don't care.* I smiled snappily, taking another step forward. *Please—can I just shower first? I don't want—* And then I smelled what he was saying and shrugged, pretending not to understand. I brought him a fresh towel and some of my own clothes and he was in the bathroom for a long time with the hot water running.

I SPENT THE NIGHT not because I saved her, but because she saved me. She fed me, she clothed me in her too-short pants and made me a blanket-nest on the couch that now faced a coffee table instead of armchairs. All the dining furniture was in the living room, and the couches and armchairs and reading lamps had been moved to the foyer, and the foyer was nowhere to be found. It was a new apartment, totally unfamiliar, like I'd never been there, like we'd never happened. It smelled like vanilla candles instead of . . . what it had smelled like before. Wood. Linseed oil, incense. Only the bathroom was exactly the same. I used her tweezers to slit the dirt from under the nails of my fingers and toes and I scrubbed my body as hard as I could to get the grease off my skin. All my clothes I washed by hand and the water ran like sewage for ten minutes straight, and I couldn't, I just couldn't go on. I threw everything except my coat under the sink. I dried myself with a towel, and in the mirror a tripod covered in skin revolved, pretending to be my body.[31] My bones were rod-thin and rod-long. I hid my scariness in her clothes and came out shivering. We hugged then, but she wouldn't let me kiss her like I used to. When I tried, she bowed her head into my chest and that was all, my hair dripping on her like a tree after good rain, and the two of us as fragile as birds. I fished out of my coat pocket a gift I had been carrying with me for weeks: a Palestinian coin from 1939 I'd found on the street, with writing in Arabic, English, and Hebrew curled around its holed middle. She seemed about to cry. She brought out a few more blankets, but didn't invite me into her bed and did not go herself. I was asleep within minutes, my head in her lap.

---

31. This is a reference to the Nubian writer Seif Deif's 1968 surrealist novella *Mourner in Space-Time Continuum*, in which the protagonist is serially metamorphosed into such varied objects as a boot, a tripod, and a tuktuk.

THE BOY FROM SHOBRAKHEIT told me he weighs fifty-eight kilograms on my bathroom scale. I fed him the food I'd cooked for William the night before and prayed he wouldn't choke on it.[32] He ate slowly, as though thinking through the quinoa. When I woke up, alone on the couch, his shoes were gone but his clothes were sopped to a pulp in a corner of the bathroom floor. I went into the bedroom but there was no sign of his having been in there. The bedsheets were twisted, just as I'd left them after my last sexcapade. William's leather jacket hung incriminatingly over the shoulders of a chair, his deodorant on the vanity, his texts lighting up the phone I'd locked in a drawer. Two nights later, the boy from Shobrakheit called (I unblocked him) asking if I was hungry. I met him at the ahwa under the bridge and we walked to a nearby alley, where I bought us sandwiches of breaded chicken and Turkish cheese fried in black oil. It was the first time since he'd reappeared that I got to look at him properly. There was an unhealthy smudge, as of pencil lead, all over his skin, and it hurt to see the gauntness of his new face. But he was in high spirits. As we ate he told me how he'd spotted the same motorcyclist we had once seen together, who drives around downtown with a man-sized Rottweiler sitting on its tail behind him, its paws on his shoulders, and how this time it stole a cigarette right out of his hand. *Who did?* I asked. *The dog,* he answered, and we cried on the ground, laughing. What is Cairo? What is life? *I swear to dog, the god stole it out of my hand!* And then he kissed the back of my hand and I had to look away. It wasn't funny anymore. I have to be gentle now that I'm refusing him. But there isn't a gentle way to say no to a man who knows he is being told no and continues in a pleading manner. We drank coffee after coffee until finally I said I

---

32. There is a superstition among Arabs that a meal prepared for a spouse or lover can turn poisonous if eaten by anyone else.

would have to go home. He wanted to walk me there and I couldn't decide if it would be crueler to stop him then or later, so I let him walk me to the gate of the building. He tried to wish me flowered dreams, dreams of honey. He tried to say these things casually but the words came out too soft as I took the shining key and unlocked the lock and said goodnight and closed the grated gate behind me.

DOES SHE NOT KNOW? Is there any possibility she doesn't know? I see her three or four times a week now, but always on my own initiative. I work her pity like a bow saw, lengthwise, violining with a hand against the bones of my own throat. When I phone, her heart can't deny me. She cancels plans with other people and we meet at the ahwa or at Zigzag and it is almost like it used to be, except that at the end of the night she goes home and I don't. But does she know this? When we part, there is always money in one of my pockets and neither of us acknowledges the transfer or the fact that I've been downgraded from lover to charity ward and am living off her beneficence like the stray dogs on Champollion. She feeds me but won't hold my body close to hers. She won't hold my body close to hers *because* she feeds me. Like the goose, all tender and no tit.[33] *Will you do me a favor?* I asked last night, reaching for her hand just as she was leaving, and I saw—it was clear to anyone—that her *yes* was full of dread at this ask that required commitment before the full measure of the ask could be revealed. It is a feint at the patron's pocket to see if her hand will flinch: a test not of her generosity but of her guilt before my boundless love. Can she trust me to toe the line, to respect what we are and what we are not, or will I ask for too much? Will my greed or, worse, my *need*—face-slapping, hair-tearing desperation—bubble to the surface and expose the charade we have been acting out since that night I failed to rescue her and was rescued myself instead? She chewed the inside of her cheek and waited to hear what I wanted from her, looking like a child about to be reprimanded. Adorable! Almost too much to bear. *Don't ever let anyone photograph you in digital,* I said, her hand still in mine, but limp and unhappy there. *Your body was made for the screech and grain of old-fashioned film.* It

33. An Egyptian saying that refers to a girl who doesn't put out despite signals to the contrary. It was popularized by the 2002 film *El-Limby*, starring Fifi Abdou.

was the first time in months that I had referenced her nudes, the nudes she still believed I had. Her breath caught in her throat like a sleeve on a door handle, as if she was only now realizing how vulnerable she might be. Was I blackmailing her? I smiled. She breathed an embarrassed sigh of relief and it was all the information I needed. There is no way she doesn't know where I go to sleep at night.

WHERE ARE YOU GOING? I asked yesterday and he buttoned his coat without looking at me and then said, *Well, you're going home, right? Work tomorrow? British Council, bright and early, fraternizing with the enemy?* It was an old joke between us and he didn't mean it to sound so bitter. Every time he speaks, even if he gets the words right, his tone outs him as a thing in pain. I tried to save him with my own levity: *Yes, that's where I'm going, but where are* you *going?* He smiled and said, *Do you need anything?* We dare each other. I dare him to answer me and he dares me to ask the question one more time. I ask again and again and he changes the subject. Yesterday, I went one further. *Are you going home?* I said. He raised his eyebrows and left without reply. At first, I saw him a few times a week but now it is almost nightly. At first, I gave him tens and twenties that he might mistake for his own, lucky change forgotten in a pocket from long ago. When he didn't object, I began to give him fifties. Then yesterday when we hugged, I slipped into his coat a thousand pounds, and he still didn't say anything. This has become our routine. We eat something cheap together and then part innocently, like we used to in the very beginning, before he ever set foot in my apartment and got comfortable there. If I want a night off I have to put my phone in airplane mode. Otherwise, if I see his call, I'll answer, and if I answer, I'll go to him. There is something I owe him, though I don't understand what, and this debt is a gentleman's tie around my neck, requiring ballroom manners, that level of care. As soon as you begin rejecting a man, you have to be twice as polite. There's a danger between us, but I'm not always sure who it belongs to. Which of us needs protection and which of us should be afraid? Tonight, my phone is in a drawer, not ringing, and every sound from the stairwell is cause for panic as William drips his sweat into my open eye, onto my exposed throat, as he shifts his grip from my shoulder to the headboard for better anchorage. I hear the whine of the elevator door and clamp my hand across his mouth instinctively. He's surprised but then his smile begins to feed from my palm like a cat. He thinks I'm playing with him. Lifting my legs over both of his shoulders, one by one, he speeds up, heaves harder. He licks between my fingers, his tongue peeping through the gaps. The fool cannot register terror on the face of a woman he is actively loving. The fear is crying from my eyes, a trail moving out across each temple, crawling down around my head until it wets the back of my scalp and the pillow beneath me. William continues to hammer at me, and the word I hear in the dark of my dissociation is *labor*: *The man is laboring at you, he hammers into you like this is his job, like he gets paid to hammer.* An attitude so different from that of the boy from Shobrakheit, who always turned off the lights or closed his eyes during sex and went somewhere far away . . . In the hallway outside the door: silence. William finishes loud and clear all over me before rolling off. The knock comes a few minutes later. By this time, William is on the balcony scrolling through his phone and I'm standing, one foot out of the bathroom, one foot in, ready to wash the stickiness off me. The smell of sex thick in the air.

BUT COCAINE GOES SO NICELY WITH MURDER. That's what Magdy said on the phone when the unthinkable happened. I was walking down Sherif Street to pay my rent at long last—two months of it, anyway—when his voice, that cream-white effeminate *Allo?* that haunts my dreams, puffed out of my jacket pocket like a spritz of perfume. I hadn't heard it in six months, since June. *Allo, allo?* The phone hadn't even rung. Disoriented, I ducked into an alley to answer, *Allo?*, and his voice was so familiar it seemed to spring from inside my own head. *How much?* he said immediately. *Magdy? Did you call me, or . . .* I checked my phone. *I'm sorry, I must have called you by mistake,* I tried to explain. *Does it matter?* he quipped. *How much?* I should have just hung up then but I tried to make conversation with him. I was desperate for an exchange of any kind, the American girl having made herself unreachable since the day before. *Funny, today of all days I have a little money on me, but actually, Magdy, it would kill me to score—* I started to say, when Magdy interrupted: *But cocaine goes so nicely with murder.*[34] He laughed and told me to meet one of his boys at the Central Bank, which was not far from where I stood at that very moment, bewildered, thinking, *Look what God has clashed together.* What are the chances I should be here at the very moment my phone remembers Magdy and chooses his number from any number of numbers, and that I should have just enough money in my pocket when it does? I've always trusted in guiding signs. After all, what kind of god would string together this many serendipities only to lure me to harm? I crossed the street, I looked alive.

---

34. In Cairo, one of the street names for cocaine rhymes with *murder*, making this a popular proverb to indicate that a user of the drug will remain one until it kills him.

IT HAPPENED. It happened as it was always going to happen, and it happened quickly. One of those moments when you are pushed outside your ordinariness into a drama where you do not belong, and the drama is full of accidents and the accidents full of repercussions that are grossly disproportionate: you strike a nail with a hammer and the whole building comes down. *Me? I was the one that caused all this?* I looked around me at the ruins and could not comprehend that they were mine. *No, please, not this.* It was excessive, imaginative, punishing in a way that only fiction could or should be. *This is the shape of narrative climax, but what is it doing in my life?* For a week afterward, I had to be told every few hours where I was, who I was, and why I was there. Reem moved into the apartment to keep me alive. And then the ifs came and they never left me. If only I had allowed the boy from Shobrakheit to call that night instead of throwing my phone into a drawer. If only I had answered the phone, even just to say no to dinner, *I'm not feeling well, I'm on a deadline with this grading,* anything at all, he would not have come to my door. And if he had *had* to come to my door, if only he had knocked and left, if only he hadn't said my name through the wood . . . But he said my name. He knocked a second time and he said my name, and I knew from hanging out the laundry that morning that it was cold outside. He was still wearing my clothes under his coat and I was not wearing my clothes at all. There was no time to save anything. He said my name, so I came to the door wearing only a T-shirt that doesn't belong to me, imagining I could deescalate the situation if I kept my body out of view, but the door banged open. He pushed right past, didn't even notice the shirt or the stink in the air. He turned into the empty bedroom. He moved to the kitchen, he moved to the living room, the bathroom, back to the bedroom like a murder-verb looking for its object, and I followed him, pleading but too afraid to reach out and touch his arm (for a moment I knew, or thought I knew, which of us the danger belonged to), back to the living room, to the dining room and its balcony, where William had just laughed out loud. It happened quickly. The boy from Shobrakheit charged at him and William, shocked in the water-glow of his phone, doubled over in time to catch his speed over the shoulder, pick it up by the knees, and tip him over the balustrade.

PART THREE

INSTRUCTOR sits at the head of the table. On his left are MINNIE, ALEX, and LAURA, and on his right are TIM, NOOR, JACQUES, and CANDICE. They are all facing one another in a loose circle with sheets of paper and pens before them. LAURA has her laptop open. CANDICE is helping JACQUES choose from among several shades of hair dye he is ordering on his phone. NOOR flips through a printout in front of her, looking bored and resigned. The lighting is fluorescent, academic, and the air-conditioning is on blast.

INSTRUCTOR   All right, everybody, it looks like it's just the seven of us today. I'm assuming you've all read the piece? [*Several nod.*] Laura, you didn't print, but did you . . . ?

LAURA   Trees.

INSTRUCTOR   *Trees*, right. That's fine, just cc me your written feedback so I have a copy. Anyone else saving the planet today? [*JACQUES and TIM shake their heads. ALEX smiles.*] Great. So we're workshopping Noor this week, part 3. Very heavy stuff. I think I speak for all of us when I say: Ouch. [*There is polite chuckling around the table.*] Noor, you want to read an excerpt for us? [*He nods as he asks the question.*] Yes? Go ahead.

NOOR   [*She picks up the stapled pages in front of her and begins to read.*] It was when I put my phone in airplane mode, permanently, that I realized there was no one left for me in Cairo. [*All begin flipping through their own papers, looking for the section being read.*] For weeks I would wake up to fifteen missed calls on my phone, from Riche, the British Council, the cleaning lady, unknown numbers that I feared were the police or worse, someone from Shobrakheit . . . I didn't answer any of them. [*ALEX pushes his page toward MINNIE, who is still flipping through her own printout, so they can share.*] The only people I wanted to talk to were the ones who Skyped or FaceTimed me anyway, because they were halfway across the world. And yet when I talked to them, there was nothing to say. I felt the ocean between us. Elijah was campaigning for Bernie Sanders, but I couldn't remember how I was supposed to react to this. Lulu had recently discovered *Love Island* and called wanting to gossip about season 2. And my mother. My mother was drinking too much . . . They had no idea what had happened to me in Cairo and I couldn't tell them. What could I possibly say? A boy is dead? A boy from a village you've never heard of is dead because of me? It would take too long to explain, and in the end I knew their verdict would be generous and unfair. I could already hear their voices, sympathizing, commiserating, assuring me against all evidence that I had done nothing wrong, refusing to listen or understand . . . The prospect of their forgiveness was as dreaded to me as the prospect of accusations from Shobrakheit. So I kept my phone in airplane mode, and when I spoke to friends and family in the States I let them tell me about their hookups, the shows they were bingeing, had I heard Drake's new single, would a man-bun suit Elijah, did I know the meme with the two Kermit frogs? Until one day my internet cut off in the middle of a sped-up Tasty video for vegan goulash. I needed to make the monthly trip to the Vodafone outlet to pay my internet bill, but I couldn't. There was no reason I couldn't, but I couldn't. I hadn't left the apartment in weeks and had been living off delivery apps that brought food to my door. The thought of facing the men on the street and at the ahwa, the doorman, the dry cleaner, the ful-maker, the kiosk-owner, the banana-seller with his cart on Champollion . . . I had even started drying my laundry on hangers in the closet so as not to have to open the balcony shutters and let in the horrible light. When the video froze, my first thought was: *Finally.* A way out. It was as though I had been waiting for a moment when I couldn't leave the building so I would have to leave the country. It occurred to me simply, that I would never need to visit another Vodafone outlet if I got on a plane to JFK. I would never need to cross eight lanes of roaring traffic, terrified for my life, only to duck into a junky taxi with no meter and no seat belt, and be lectured the whole ride about the religious rulings against cross-dressing and the importance of women looking like women. I would never again need to be asked by a waiter or a plumber or a stranger why I had a buzz cut and where I was from. I would never need to struggle to explain myself in Arabic or be followed by street children selling tissues, calling me a faggot. If I wanted to, I could never again see anyone who had heard of the boy from Shobrakheit or anyone who'd heard of Shobrakheit in the first place. I could just call Egyptair and book a flight home. [*NOOR finishes reading and continues to stare at the page for several seconds before flipping the print-out back to the beginning.*]

INSTRUCTOR   Mm-hmm ... [*He pauses respectfully.*] Thank you for reading that, Noor. Good choice of excerpt, and such an emotional delivery. Really very moving.

CANDICE   Yeah. Hearing it out loud is so powerful. [*to NOOR*] I was reading this last night in bed and kept wanting to call you and just be like, *Are you okay?* [*Several people around the room nod.*] I mean, I know this happened over a year ago and you mentioned last time you're in therapy, but I can't get over how traumatic this must have been for you.

ALEX   Yeah. And to go through it all alone.

CANDICE   You must have been relieved when he died—I know that sounds horrible.

LAURA   It's not horrible, it's realistic.

CANDICE   Yeah. My aunt Lemma was married to her abuser for fourteen years, and even after he went to prison for assaulting Darnell—that's her son, they have two sons—she still couldn't sleep because she was terrified he'd get out or send someone to the house to kill her. She moved halfway across the country and wouldn't tell anyone where. She used to call us from pay phones like it was the nineties. Anyway, her insomnia only went away when she got to see the body.

LAURA   Makes sense, honestly.

ALEX   Wait—how did he die?

CANDICE   Uh, knifing, I think. [*turning from ALEX to NOOR*] But what I'm trying to say is it's so brave of you to return to this place and really excavate while the ground is still wet. For a lot of people, it takes longer.

INSTRUCTOR I think we can all agree with that. It can't be easy to revisit these memories, but I hope—and feel quite certain—that this is the best way for you to process your time in Cairo, the violence of your relationship with . . . the deceased. Give it language, take ownership. But [*smiles*] why don't we get going? As usual, once everyone is done giving their feedback, Noor, you'll have a chance to respond to any comments, or ask questions of your own. [*He winks at NOOR.*] Please refrain from jumping in until then so you can hear the impressions of your readers without paratextual input. [*He looks around the room.*] Right, Minnie, let's start with you. You always have something to say.

            [*CANDICE, JACQUES, and ALEX smile.*]

MINNIE   Right, so the ending isn't working for me at all.

[*All laugh.*]

MINNIE   No, really. I know you all think I have a problem with every submission, but that's not true. No, seriously—

INSTRUCTOR   Guys, let her finish, please.

[*They quiet down.*]

MINNIE   I mean, part 1 was structurally weird enough, what with no paragraphs and the perspective flipping back and forth . . . It was really hard to follow, plot-wise, and just left so many questions unanswered— literally—these questions that have nothing to do with the actual events, and I know Noor wanted it to be—

INSTRUCTOR   Hey, hey, let's try *not* assigning intent this time.

MINNIE   Okay, well, whatever the intention, it just feels unnecessary. Like, I get it. She's trying to experiment with form. But you can't be swapping voices that frequently *and* jumping around temporally and then *also* have these koan-riddles at the top of every page. Why are we even getting his voice in *your* memoir? [*to NOOR*] How does that even make sense? You in the boy's head like that when the whole point is that you don't fully get each other, you're from different worlds, et cetera . . . You said last time you were trying to humanize him, but honestly, for me, all these alarm bells start going off, like I just become suspicious. And I *know* you. If I didn't, like if I just picked this up at a bookstore . . . it's asking a lot from readers you've never met. Especially when there are logistical obstacles and inconsistencies we're expected to just swallow, like: How do you know he was stalking you if in the memoir *you didn't know he was stalking you*? Same thing with the drugs and rape-fantasies. You said he made up things about Cairo and his family all the time just to mess with you, but then you carry on reporting what you heard so we don't know what to believe, like, are we getting the fact-checked version or . . . ? Everything is potentially tainted—*especially* when the footnotes come in. Obviously, I'm not trying to tell you about your own culture, but I googled a few of them and—

INSTRUCTOR   I don't mean to interrupt you, Minnie, but we did talk about the footnotes last time, and also the alternating voices. I'm wondering if you have any thoughts on the *third* part, the last part.

MINNIE   I'm getting there, I swear. [*INSTRUCTOR puts his hands up in playful surrender.*] My whole point is just that in parts 1 and 2, having to maintain this level of skepticism the whole time . . . you're really hoping for a big, fat payoff as a reader. To justify all that labor, you know? I was waiting on the third part to bring everything together, give me that aha moment, but in the end . . . I just found myself even *more* confused. I don't mean to sound rude, but why were you grieving so much? There was so much guilt, and I kept thinking, *Am I missing something? Did I misread the balcony scene? Did you push him or something?* I kept—

LAURA   [*under her breath*] Wow.

                 [*Several people look aghast.*]

MINNIE   —going back and checking if there was a confession I missed somewhere. And then why didn't his family come to claim the body? What kind of a family would take this news over the phone? [*These questions are directed at NOOR, who, because of the gag rule in workshop, cannot answer.*] There were just so many basic plot points that were unclear, and after enduring all the experimentation of parts 1 and 2, flipping backward and forward, I was really hoping all my acrobatics would pay off. But they didn't. They just didn't.

ALEX   Can I step in?

INSTRUCTOR   Please.

ALEX   Well, I don't want to harp on, because we talked about this so much when we did part 2. But I just want to repeat that I'm Team Footnotes. Really glad you took our advice after the first workshop and added some stage whispers for us. If anything, they made me trust you even *more*. I didn't have the same skepticism thing as Minnie going on, just really enjoyed the intel on Middle Eastern culture.

LAURA   Same.

ALEX   And, like, vaginal teeth—whoa. Amazing. I think
             if anything we should get more of those friendly
             asides, and maybe also more sensory detail? After
             all this time, I still don't know what downtown
             Cairo looks like. Is it skyscrapers? Are there mar-
             kets or malls? What are the women wearing in
             the street? And, like, the village Shobrakeet—
             [shrugs] I can't picture it at all. You have to remem-
             ber we have zero references, so unless we're given
             a shit-ton of description, we're *probably* going to
             get it wrong. And how sad—like, what a waste
             that would be. As an Egyptian, you have access
             to a culture we never get to experience at this
             proximity—in English, I mean, straight from the
             source—so there's real opportunity for . . . I don't
             know, excess? [*He tosses a handful of imaginary con-
             fetti.*] I think you can afford to celebrate more of
             the little stuff that's *un*googleable, all those tex-
             tures and kinks that make Cairo, Cairo. You're al-
             ready using some of them in the footnotes, I just
             think there's room for more. But, anyway, yeah . . .
             Part 3 . . . my issue with part 3 is tied to my issue
             with the work as a whole, and it has to do with the
             emotional investment we have in the characters,
             especially the boy from Shobrakeet—we still don't
             know his name, right? Or did I miss that? [*He flips
             through his pages.*]

MINNIE   No, we *don't* know his name, and that's another ex-
             ample of the confusion I'm talking about. Like, we

really need something solid to hold on to here—
[*looks exasperatedly around at everyone*] But, sorry,
Alex, go on.

JACQUES [*to INSTRUCTOR*] But can she even say his name?

INSTRUCTOR What—legally?

JACQUES Well.

MINNIE Either way, though, she could give him a fake
name.

INSTRUCTOR Legally, the dead are fair game in most states.

MINNIE [*to NOOR*] So you *could* name him, really. Call him
anything. Call him Ahmed.

INSTRUCTOR But even if he were alive, so long as the account is
honest, so long as it is *descriptive* rather than mali-
cious, you have nothing to fear. Legally speaking,
there is only one rule: if you write anything nega-
tive about a living person, it better be true. For
stories of abuse, the victim—or *survivor*, as we say
now [*looks pleased with himself*]—has every right to
tell her story.

TIM Or his.

INSTRUCTOR Or his! Right you are, Tim. His, her. *They*. Juries
are extremely sympathetic to victim testimonies
even without tangible evidence. There is an im-

plicit understanding that accounts of abuse are . . . most likely true. Success rates for defamation suits are very, very low. They are also—I mean. Well. It's expensive to take someone to court, so that's another barrier. Usually celebrities can, high-profile politicians, but otherwise . . .

JACQUES   Right, so.

ALEX   Right.

MINNIE   Fat chance for him.

INSTRUCTOR   [*to ALEX*] But you were saying?

ALEX   Right, I was trying to say the boy from Shobrakeet isn't too sympathetic from the beginning.

LAURA   He's abusive.

ALEX   Exactly. I just found it hard to grieve for him in the way that the speaker does in part 3. All her guilt feels a bit alien to me. Which is, I think, what Minnie was also trying to say.

MINNIE   Yeah.

LAURA   I agree one hundred percent. I'm not saying the Shobrakit guy deserved to die, but I think he did it to himself. His chauvinism was killing him from the beginning. The first time they're alone together, he rapes her—

CANDICE   [*nodding to NOOR*] You said no.

LAURA   —and even after that, he was oozing toxic mascu-
                 linity and red flag behavior. I mean, all of part 2 is
                 about him becoming a stalker. And then suddenly
                 he dies and she's all brokenhearted . . . Obviously,
                 I'm not trying to tell you how to feel [*to NOOR*],
                 but he was so manipulative even when you two
                 were together: leeching off you, isolating you from
                 the people that cared about you . . . I don't think
                 you owe him that heartbreak. I'm not sure how you
                 can position yourself in this work, but I think it
                 needs to be clearer that you're not responsible for
                 what happened. Especially today, considering the
                 moment we're living in, with #MeToo, and Brett
                 Kavanaugh a few months ago . . . I just think we
                 have to be really careful about the stories we tell
                 and where we cue for violins. Who are we asking
                 the audience to identify with? How do we manage
                 blame? I don't know about you guys, but person-
                 ally, I was relieved when the Shobrakit guy died. I
                 mean, this is a man that was entertaining the most
                 violent fantasies about you. [*to NOOR*] And then
                 told you! Or at least I'm assuming—how else could
                 you know? He spent months spying on you, follow-
                 ing you to and from work, trying to engineer a
                 life-threatening situation just so he could swoop
                 in and save you . . . He blackmailed you with your
                 own nudes.

CANDICE   Revenge porn.

ALEX   He also stole from you.

INSTRUCTOR   Do we know that he stole from her?

LAURA   He totally stole from her. How else could he have
              paid for that first relapse? When he goes up on the
              bridge?

MINNIE   Wait, he stole what?

              [*LAURA rolls her eyes involuntarily.*]

ALEX   [*in a hushed voice to MINNIE*] We're talking about
              the pearls.

LAURA   And also, if you think about what took the Shobrakit
              guy up to her apartment in the first place—I mean
              the night he dies. He went up there because he found
              out she was sleeping with William. He was going
              to *murder* William when he accidentally fell off the
              balcony himself.

MINNIE   How did he find out about William?

ALEX   She's extrapolating.

LAURA   [*frowns*] It's in the language, Minnie.

MINNIE   Well, I just think that's the sort of thing that needs
              to be clear. If half of the people reading don't re-
              alize that the guy is a thief and a murderer, that's a

problem. [*LAURA opens her mouth, but MINNIE plows on.*] It's a problem *in the language.*

INSTRUCTOR   Thank you, Minnie, I think you've made your point! Can we return to the question of the speaker's grief for a moment? I want to remind everyone that this is memoir, not fiction, and it is the special power of memoir to archive our most private personal dramas—for which there is often no other place of safekeeping. Meaning, you don't have to *approve* of how the writer remembers or processes the death of someone she knew. We are not here to therapize. We are here to listen and bear witness.

CANDICE   That's exactly, *exactly,* what I wanted to say. There's no wrong way to feel. When someone *falls off your balcony and dies*, you're entitled to whatever coping mechanism works for you.

LAURA   Well . . .

CANDICE   Every response is equally valid.

LAURA   Well, sure, but if a victim resorts to self-harm or self-blame—

CANDICE   She's allowed to *write* about it. She shouldn't have to pretend it didn't happen.

LAURA   Candice, that's not what I mean. I'm actually on your side. Also, sorry [*raises her hand with the elbow resting on the table and looks at INSTRUCTOR*], can I disagree for a moment with something you said?

INSTRUCTOR   Of course! [*beaming*]

LAURA   Okay, so. Last year when Mac Miller overdosed, everyone blamed Ariana Grande for breaking up with him, saying she pushed him over the edge. Everyone *knew* he suffered from addiction but still held her responsible for allowing him to die. And that reaction didn't just come from nowhere, there's a whole precedent in the literature, in the media. Like the way tabloids talk about women—and it's not just tabloids, I mean, it's a bigger problem, obviously. But we demand all this emotional labor from them. We reward loyalty and punish women for choosing independence—for choosing *survival*, actually.

CANDICE   [*softly*] Hmm.

LAURA   There's this script. Like a social script. And it keeps women trapped in these destructive relationships because they feel guilty leaving. I just think as writers, we have a hand in shaping that. I'm not saying we should all write manuals, like how-to-leave-your-boyfriend or get-out-alive . . . but at the same time our writing isn't just floating in the ether [*mimes a butterfly with one hand*]. We need to hold each other accountable for the narratives we perpetuate. Don't get me wrong—I love this memoir project, I think it's so, so important. But if we're going to have this account of a girl who blames herself for the death of her depressive, possessive, extremely *violent* ex, I don't think it's too much to ask for a little more self-interrogation. Like, where does that guilt come from and is it fair to her? [*turns to NOOR*] Are you being fair to *yourself*?

CANDICE   Yeah, I totally get what you're saying now. The rape too. We don't really get enough of that.

LAURA   Exactly. It's like she suggests it, but then doesn't address it head-on. The last thing you want your reader wondering is *if* you were raped. It just undermines the whole . . . I mean, there's an ethical dimension here. We can talk about craft forever, but we also have to ask: Is a narrative like this [*nodding at her laptop*] normalizing cycles of abuse? Is it perpetuating misogyny?

          [*There is an impressed moment of silence. CANDICE nods slowly.*]

INSTRUCTOR   All good points! [*He looks around at them all, beaming still.*]

TIM   [*clears throat and says politely to LAURA*] If this had happened to you, how would you grieve?

LAURA   Personally? I would grieve as though my psychotic stalker-rapist had just died before he could kill anyone else. But I'm not even saying Noor isn't allowed to feel bad. I just think she was probably also relieved on some level. And I couldn't find her relief on the page.

INSTRUCTOR   Tim, why don't you go next, seeing as you asked the question? Or Jacques can go, if you need a minute to collect yourself.

[*TIM jumps a little and looks around at JACQUES, then at INSTRUCTOR, unsure who to address.*]

TIM   Me? Should I go?

INSTRUCTOR   Please.

TIM   [*He clears his throat again and looks down at his papers before speaking very quietly.*] I didn't really write any comments about the speaker or her grief. I was more interested in her friends from the café.

[*INSTRUCTOR nods encouragingly.*]

TIM   Well, so in part 3, after the boy from Shobrakheit falls off the balcony, there's this whole dark, self-loathing period. [*He begins to tick events off his fingers.*] The speaker tells William she never wants to see him again. Then Reem moves into the apartment to take care of her when she stops eating. Sammy also starts coming by the apartment to check in on them both. And within a few days she finds out Sammy and Reem started a rumor that the balcony-death was a suicide. Then she cuts them out of her life too—

ALEX   They don't really *start* the rumor.

              [*TIM's ears flush immediately.*]

INSTRUCTOR   Please, Alex, let him finish.

ALEX   Sorry.

INSTRUCTOR   [*nods and smiles, mouthing to ALEX*] It's fine.

TIM   I just mean—I mean when the crowd gathers around
              the body, the two of them start telling everyone he
              was just some homeless guy, just a junkie who prob-
              ably jumped off the roof. It's all just—you know,
              it's a bit unfair. What people start saying about the
              Shobrakheit boy.

CANDICE   He *was* a junkie, though.

TIM   Well.

CANDICE   And homeless.

TIM   Right.

CANDICE   I think it's important to just—like, to call a thing
              what it is. If he was sleeping in the mosque, he was
              homeless. If he was shooting coke, that's a junkie.
              It's not some exaggeration meant to discredit his
              life. It's, like, a truth of his life? A straight-up fact?
              And hard enough to admit about someone you loved.
              [*Her voice cracks a little and the room goes quiet.*]

TIM   Honestly, I didn't mean—

CANDICE   And maybe this is a race thing. Like maybe that's
             why I'm taking this so . . . I just think, as a woman
             of color who's been *systemically* gaslit by men my
             whole life, I think being honest with ourselves
             and naming even those we are closest to helps us
             see them, and see ourselves? Especially when it's a
             Black man, or whatever, Arab, Muslim, there's
             this whole—there's just so much stereotype. Like
             you don't want to call the cops, because they al-
             ready hate Black people—my aunt Lemma, it took
             years and even then—you don't want to admit he
             was a crackhead, because it's what the reader ex-
             pects. And you want them to be wrong. But also.
             Sometimes they're not wrong. And you're only
             hurting yourself when you hide the truth. It's
             like what Laura was saying about women. Part of
             what keeps us in these patterns is the feeling that
             our abuser is unique? That he's not like others?
             And we have to protect him from the judgment
             of a world that doesn't understand [*close to tears*],
             when actually . . .

TIM   [*very flustered*] Definitely, no, you're right. I'm not
             saying he wasn't any of those things.

CANDICE   It's not your job to prove he was good? When you're
             honest about the person, even if the drugs are part
             of that, you have to, you just have to . . .

TIM   I see your point, really. I was— I mean, I was think-
               ing more of Sammy and Reem. But I see your point,
               totally.

               [*There is an uncomfortable pause while TIM tries des-*
               perately to make eye contact with CANDICE.]

INSTRUCTOR   *Okayyy.* I realize this is a very personal topic for
               many of us [*CANDICE stares at the door*], but I'd
               like to invite everyone to take a deep breath and
               remember that it can be as difficult to *share* as it
               is to *receive.* [*MINNIE gives him a small interruptive*
               wave.] Yes, Minnie.

MINNIE   I get what Candice is saying, but the drugs still
               didn't make sense to me. How is he a cocaine addict
               and also that poor?

INSTRUCTOR   [*smiles kindly*] Good question. Maybe we need more
               info about the price of cocaine in Cairo.

LAURA   You know [*to TIM*], I realize Sammy and Reem
               didn't intentionally start the rumor about the sui-
               cide, but I think the boy from Shobrakeet had a
               death wish anyway.

ALEX   Yeah, I was just going to say. It's actually the clos-
               est version to the truth they could give an angry
               mob in that moment. They even explained after-
               ward that it's only by bringing up the drugs that
               they were protecting Noor from accusations of
               murder—

LAURA   And William.

ALEX   Both of them. They're the only witnesses, and the
               case is already weird enough: a random white guy
               and this Egyptian girl on a tourist visa claim a home-
               less guy was in their house—

LAURA   Apartment.

ALEX   Right, some apartment belonging to some German
               academic, and the homeless guy fell from the bal-
               cony and died . . . Who's gonna buy that? The whole
               neighborhood shows up and no one buys that. Im-
               mediately it's that mob mentality, everybody shout-
               ing, fucking *machetes* come out, they've got William
               by the neck. And the police are totally useless, ready
               to arrest anyone . . . [*to NOOR*] Maybe we need
               more cultural context here? But I think it helps to re-
               member that this is not Manhattan. It's downtown
               Cairo. Military state. There's political tension . . . It
               could turn into a bloodbath, easily. So, like, I under-
               stand why Sammy and Reem start telling people
               about the drugs. They might have saved Noor's
               life, actually, or spared her, whatever . . . months in
               prison. I feel like they knew what they were doing.

INSTRUCTOR   Okay, *interesting* . . . Tim, where were you going
               with your point about Sammy and Reem? I want to
               let you finish before we get swept away.

TIM   Well. [*He glances nervously at LAURA's laptop.
               CANDICE is still death-staring the door.*] Well, I see

Alex and Laura's point, but I still—I just didn't feel it was fair what they said about him. Even if it was true. Even if it was . . . you know, tactical. The rumor might have been helping Noor, but it was hurting the Shobrakheit boy more than he deserved to be hurt. [*He frowns.*] They flattened him.

INSTRUCTOR   So you weren't too sympathetic toward Sammy and Reem?

TIM   No, I thought they were the problem, maybe. And . . . I can understand why Noor cut them off when she heard what they'd been saying. And why she went a little . . . you know. Her guilt makes sense to me. It starts with the rumor, not with the accident. She doesn't feel responsible for the boy's death, she feels responsible for his character assassination [*glances at NOOR*], I *think*. Sammy and Reem, they made him out to be totally worthless, like just a nobody they didn't know, had never sat or smoked with, someone who didn't even deserve a proper police investigation and that—actually, *that's* the problem. Maybe Noor *should* have been interrogated for murder. [*CANDICE's head snaps in TIM's direction.*] Maybe she *needed* to be investigated even if she was innocent. Maybe . . . the fact that the police don't even suspect her or William, like, says something about why he died.

CANDICE   [*in disbelief*] Well, your alliances are clear as fucking daylight.

TIM   No, no—

CANDICE   Arrest the survivor?

TIM   I didn't mean it like that.

CANDICE   Have you ever been stalked? Blackmailed?

TIM   No, you're right—

CANDICE   Have you ever had furniture thrown at you? Have
             you ever been raped?

TIM   It was just a thought about—

CANDICE   I'm so *tired* of men.

             [*She tilts her head back and blinks at the ceiling, looking
             truly exhausted. There's another uncomfortable silence
             during which TIM looks at INSTRUCTOR pleadingly.*]

JACQUES   Same.

             [*CANDICE is the only one who laughs, but this defuses
             the tension considerably. JACQUES puts an arm around
             her and his earring immediately catches in her hair. They
             spend several moments disentangling.*]

ALEX   [*quietly to TIM*] You were talking about class?

TIM   [*He looks at ALEX with a bewildered expression as though
             surprised anyone had been listening.*] Yes.

[*CANDICE sniffs loudly.*]

TIM   Power and . . . yeah, class.

MINNIE   [*looking from TIM to ALEX*] Are we saying Noor
               killed him?

LAURA   Metaphor, Minnie.

MINNIE   'Cause if anyone killed him—and I'm not saying
               anyone did—but if anyone killed him, it was William,
               right? [*She lowers her head like a bull and bucks.*] He
               sort of picked him up and sent him over the bal-
               cony, right? Isn't that how the boy from—I'm not
               even going to try to say it. The village boy, isn't that
               how he dies?

INSTRUCTOR   [*hastily*] How *do* we feel about William? Good of
               you to bring him up, Minnie. I don't think we've
               talked about William much or his role in the bal-
               cony scene . . .

LAURA   I don't know . . . white, cis-het, British male, walk-
               ing around like he owns everything. It's not clear
               what he's even doing in Cairo?

ALEX   Colonial vibes, for sure.

TIM   Maybe it's not clear what Noor was doing there
               either?

LAURA   What's *wrong* with you today?

INSTRUCTOR   [*quickly*] Jacques, what do *you* think about William? We haven't heard your voice much.

[*LAURA and CANDICE exchange a look of disbelief.*]

JACQUES   Mon dieu.

[*Several laugh and INSTRUCTOR is visibly relieved.*]

INSTRUCTOR   Well, I'm glad we agree on something at last! Anything you'd like to add to that?

JACQUES   [*He waits for others to finish laughing before speaking.*] Just a few things. For me there was also too much labor . . . I think paragraphs would be good. Why not? Some quotation marks, maybe? To make the dialogue easier to follow, because italicization—it is not always enough. The switching voices . . . [*frowns and tilts his head from side to side*] sometimes clear, sometimes no.

MINNIE   [*raises hand in vote*] Hard agree, oh my god.

JACQUES   But my main feedback is . . . we do not need the third part.

INSTRUCTOR   Oh?

JACQUES   It is very difficult to follow such a climax as the balcony-death. From the beginning it was like a thriller. We were, how you say, holding our breath. Why not end there? At the top? [*He mimes an airplane taking off with one hand.*] Then the subject is clear. It is not about Cairo, it is a deadly romance. Like *Giovanni's Room.*

[*INSTRUCTOR raises his eyebrows and looks around at the rest of the group, who all look at one another in turn. TIM in particular is noticeably excited.*]

INSTRUCTOR   Tim?

TIM   I think that would be respectful to . . . both parties.

[*CANDICE shakes her head.*]

INSTRUCTOR   Laura?

LAURA   Well, I think *respect* is irrelevant here. But if losing part 3 means we don't normalize victim-blaming, I'm all for it. Better to let the events speak for themselves.

CANDICE   So long as we keep the event of his death.

INSTRUCTOR   Candice? Go ahead.

CANDICE   I just think we need to see it. Like, the description of the body—that whole part with the angles of the bones. As someone who was deeply triggered by the scenes of abuse and sextortion, that closure was important for me. Just knowing Noor is finally safe . . .

LAURA   Yes.

ALEX   Yeah, it's a pretty radical suggestion, but now that
               you've mentioned it, Jacques, I think I agree that
               part 3 doesn't add much.

JACQUES   It makes the manuscript less . . . [*opens and closes his
               palms like two halves of a book*] symmetrical.

ALEX   Can I just say [*turns to JACQUES*], you always have
               such extreme revisionist suggestions—like, here's
               what you don't know about your own work [*imi-
               tating JACQUES's accent*]: Charlie is one Cher video
               away from transitioning, the mother ran over the
               dog on purpose, and the whole thing should be re-
               written as a libretto! [*All laugh.*] But I appreciate it.

INSTRUCTOR   I think we *all* do.

MINNIE   I still think having two voices doesn't make sense.

INSTRUCTOR   O-kay, then [*buoyantly, ignoring MINNIE*]. If no-
               body else has anything to add, we can turn it over
               to the writer herself, who has some very excit-
               ing news. May I? [*winks again at NOOR, who looks
               uncomfortable*] I received a call this morning that
               Noor has been offered a publishing deal for this
               manuscript—*this one* [*smacks the copy in front of him*]
               that we've been reading for six months.

CANDICE   Woo!

[*There are expressions of excitement and low hooting from everyone. No one looks happier than INSTRUCTOR.*]

ALEX   [*smiling*] Not surprised.

INSTRUCTOR   She wasn't going to say anything but I *insisted*. To remind us all that good things can come from our grimmest hours. That if we face our traumas and trust in the healing power of narrative, we can produce work that is valuable—even *marketable*. [*He snorts to indicate the joke.*] But seriously [*more seriously to NOOR*], though you are just beginning your journey with this memoir, the fact that you have already managed to touch so many readers is a testament to your fortitude as much as to your craft. It would have been easy to leave Cairo behind forever, but instead you continue to return there every day, to remember the city, the violence, and the boy himself, who is the dark heart of your book . . . Almost worth it now, wouldn't you say?

ACKNOWLEDGMENTS

Thank you first and foremost to the Graywolf pack, but especially to Anni Liu and Fiona McCrae for their tireless collaboration on this book. It has been a dream to work with such sensitive readers whose instincts I trust wholeheartedly.

Thank you to the powers behind the Disquiet Prize in Fiction and the Graywolf Press African Fiction Prize, in particular writer and judge A. Igoni Barrett, who saw something in this manuscript worth salvaging. Thank you to the Canada Council for the Arts for providing me with some financial security during the writing process and to *Granta* for publishing an excerpt of this novel in 2019. Thank you to Michelle Henry, chair of the Department of Rhetoric and Composition at the American University in Cairo, for supporting equally my writing and my teaching.

Thank you to the many dear friends who read early drafts of this book: Youssef Rakha, André Babyn, André Forget, Neil Surkan, and Mariam Bazeed. Thank you again and always to Professor Ato Quayson, my mentor and motivator, who trained me to prize a beautiful question above any answer. Thank you to Anne Michaels for her warmth and generosity. Thank you to Joud Alkorani, who keeps me. Thank you to Mariam Elnozahy, who is enough of an American girl and a boy from Shobrakheit to walk with me through this novel, suspicious of every word. Thank you to Robin Moger for being my confidante, my cheerleader, and my friend. Thank you to my family for their indefatigable support, and to my grandmother in particular, who I love more than anyone.

Thank you to Moataz Ibrahim for making Cairo home.

NOOR NAGA is an Alexandrian writer who was born in Philadelphia, raised in Dubai, studied in Toronto, and now lives in Cairo. She is author of the verse novel *Washes, Prays*, and the winner of the Bronwen Wallace Award for Emerging Writers, the RBC/PEN Canada New Voices Award, the Disquiet Prize in Fiction, and the Pat Lowther Memorial Award. She teaches at the American University in Cairo.

ABOUT THE GRAYWOLF PRESS AFRICAN FICTION PRIZE

The Graywolf Press African Fiction Prize is awarded to a first novel manuscript by an author primarily residing in Africa. Founded in 2017 to facilitate direct access to publishing in the United States for a new generation of African writers, the prize is awarded every other year. Winners receive publication by Graywolf Press and an advance.

Submissions must be full-length, previously unpublished novel manuscripts, either originally written in English or a complete English translation. If the submission is a translation, the translator need not live in Africa and the original-language book may be previously published. Agents are welcome to submit manuscripts for consideration. For more details, visit www.graywolfpress.org /submissions.

Previous winner:
The House of Rust by Khadija Abdalla Bajaber (2017)

A. Igoni Barrett, the prize judge for the 2017–2021 prize cycles, is the author of the acclaimed novel *Blackass* and the story collection *Love Is Power, or Something Like That*. He is the recipient of fellowships from the Chinua Achebe Center and the Norman Mailer Center, as well as a Rockefeller Foundation Bellagio Center residency. He lives in Nigeria.

The text of *If an Egyptian Cannot Speak English* is set in Crimson Text.
Book design by Rachel Holscher.
Composition by Bookmobile Design and Digital
Publisher Services, Minneapolis, Minnesota.

9 781644 450819